Dornford Yates is the pseudony ___
into a middle-class Victorian _____, his parents scraped
together enough money to send him to Harrow. The son of a
solicitor, he qualified for the Bar but gave up legal work in favour
of his great passion for writing. As a consequence of education
and experience, Yates' books feature the genteel life, a nostalgic
glimpse at Edwardian decadence and a number of swindling
solicitors. In his heyday and as a testament to the fine writing
in his novels, Dornford Yates' work was placed in the bestseller
list. Indeed, 'Berry' is one of the great comic creations of
twentieth-century fiction, and 'Chandos' titles were successfully
adapted for television.

Finding the English climate utterly unbearable, Yates chose
to live in the French Pyrénées for eighteen years before moving
on to Rhodesia where he died in 1960.

ADÈLE AND CO.
AND BERRY CAME TOO
AS BERRY AND I WERE SAYING
B-BERRY AND I LOOK BACK
BERRY AND CO.
THE BERRY SCENE
BLOOD ROYAL
THE BROTHER OF DAPHNE
COST PRICE
THE COURTS OF IDLENESS
EYE FOR A TOOTH
FIRE BELOW
GALE WARNING
THE HOUSE THAT BERRY BUILT
JONAH AND CO.
NE'ER DO WELL
PERISHABLE GOODS
RED IN THE MORNING
SHE FELL AMONG THIEVES
SHE PAINTED HER FACE

DORNFORD YATES

BLIND
CORNER

HOUSE OF
STRATUS

This edition published in 2001 by House of Stratus, an imprint of Stratus Books Ltd, 21 Beeching Park, Kelly Bray, Cornwall, PL17 8QS, UK.

www.houseofstratus.com

Typeset, printed and bound by House of Stratus.

A catalogue record for this book is available from the British Library and the Library of Congress.

ISBN 1-84232-967-7

To Norman Kenneth Stephen, late Senior Assistant Master of Harrow School, who was the first to show me that, though few can bend it, the long bow of English is on every man's back, this book is respectfully and gratefully dedicated.

Contents

1

The Well-digger's Statement

When the first of these things happened, that is to say upon the twentieth day of April, I was twenty-two years old, a little stronger than most men of my age, and very ready for anything that bade fair to prove more exciting than entering the office of my uncle, who was a merchant of consequence in the City of London.

I had lately been sent down from Oxford for using some avowed communists as many thought they deserved, and, though George Hanbury – for he had been with me in the affair – and I received much sympathy and more complimentary letters from complete strangers than we could conveniently answer, I think we were both more distressed than we would have cared to admit to take our leave of Christ Church before our time. For my part, I had been glad to get out of England and to put the matter as far away from my mind as ever I knew.

I had, then, spent five weeks at Biarritz, the guest of some people called Pomeroy, with whom, such was their benevolence, I believe I might have stayed indefinitely; but a letter from Hanbury, with whom I was to share a flat, threatening to forgo the agreement if I did not return to Town, at length precipitated my departure.

I returned as I had come, alone in my car, making for Dieppe and spending the first night at Angoulême and the second at Tours.

From Tours to Dieppe is a comfortable day's run, and I rose that April morning, intending to pass my third night on the packet which should take me to England.

I left Tours about ten in the morning and came to Chartres at one. There I purchased my luncheon and, after taking in petrol, re-entered the car, for the weather was very fair, and I meant to eat by the way.

Accordingly, a few miles farther, I stopped by the side of the road, and, leaving the car, sat down on a grassy bank to eat my meal.

It was a fine, smooth day, and the sunshine seemed almost as hot as it had been at Biarritz. The world, so far as I could see, I had to myself. The road stretched white and empty and straight for miles upon either hand.

I was never much of a trencherman when I had to eat alone, and my meal – a *pâté de Chartres* and some fruit, and a bottle of beer – was soon done; but, since I had plenty of time and the beer had made me heavy, I lay down in the warm grass and went to sleep.

I now know that I must have slept for near fifty minutes before I was awakened by the voices of two men, who were somewhere quite close to me. They were speaking English, and from the speech and the tone of one of them, it was clear that his temper was out of hand.

"*You*, by hell," he was crying, and I think it was the bitterness and the enmity with which he kept investing the pronoun that brought me so wide awake. "*You*. And who are *you*? *You* choose, do you? And what about us? Seven years I've done – seven years out of my life. And the others – "

"Your confinement," said the other coolly, "seems to have affected your brain. The secret's mine, and you know it. Why, because you've been in prison, should I make it over to you?"

"Because we're partners," blurted the first. I could hear him swallow. "That's why."

"Partners?" said the other. He laughed lightly. "Let me refresh your memory. For five years I led you, Ellis – you and the other four. I gave you two-thirds of every cent we took. Then, one day, you struck. You demanded five-sixths. When I refused, you swore you'd work on your own – with what result we know." He laughed again. "So much for partnership. And, then, two points," he continued: "first – that I had the secret before ever I saw your face, and, second – *that at your trial you tried to save yourself by letting me in.*"

I cannot describe the contempt with which these last words were uttered, and Ellis was plainly stung, for he let out a volley of protest, declaring that it was not he that had done it, and that the papers had reported the matter wrong.

"I was in Court," said the other, and laughed again. Then I heard him yawn. "And so, you see," he continued, "you can't be surprised that I don't jump at the chance of making you free of a fortune at my expense."

I had at first been astonished that I could hear so perfectly, for I was sure that the speakers were upon the opposite side of the bank. Then I perceived that I had my ear to a drain which must give directly into the wood beyond, and that, if I was minded to listen, I was ideally placed. But I could, of course, see nothing, and to hear, yet not to see, these two fellows was more than I could endure. I therefore rose from my gully and made my way by inches to the grass which was growing long upon the top of the bank. Into this I passed, like a snake, with the utmost caution, for I could now hear the voices almost as loud as before, and in a moment I was looking down upon two men, who were standing in a miniature glade, with the wood thick about them, and the bank upon which I was lying blocking the hither end.

The one was dressed in old tweeds, that had been well cut: he was a slight, handsome man, and wore a fair, close-cut beard: his eyes were grey and steady: he looked a gentleman. His arms were folded, and he was leaning against a tree, lazily regarding the other as though he were unclean.

The latter was a big, coarse man, soon to be fat. He was flashily dressed, with a slip to his waistcoat, and cloth-topped, patent-leather boots; and all his clothes argued an elegant taste like that of a blackamoor. His mouth was brutal, and his small, black eyes were set close in his head, and I remember wondering how two so different men could ever have agreed together for so long as five years.

Ellis was trembling with rage.

"You see," said the other, "there's really no more to be said. For the moment, so far as I am concerned, the treasure of Wagensburg will stay where it is. Whether later on I shall lift it, I really don't know; but, if I do, that I shall seek your assistance, Ellis, is most improbable. Of course, you're at liberty to go and look for yourself. You know where it is – to within some four or five miles," and, with that, he took out tobacco and started to fill a pipe.

I had never thought of such blasphemy as that which his words provoked. Ellis spouted imprecations, at once so dreadful and couched in such filthy terms that, had he then and there fallen dead, it would have seemed to me the natural con-sequence of such iniquity.

The other heard him out, busy with his pipe. Then –

"Eloquent as ever," he said. "Can you find your own way back? Oh, and by the way," he went on, not waiting for any reply, "don't come here again, or anywhere that I am. I have no use for you, and I dislike your company."

He whistled as though for some dog and started to stroll down the glade, pausing for a moment to bring a match to his pipe, and commanding my great admiration by his insolent scorn of the other's violent and menacing demeanour.

I was, indeed, in the act of admiration when the murder was done.

As the other hunched his shoulders above his pipe, Ellis struck him high up to the right of the spine, and, either from the force of the blow or from the wound, the other fell down on his face with a knife in his back.

The murderer staggered across him and nearly fell over the body, bringing himself up against a tree on the far side, panting with stress. So he stayed for a second, with his knees loose and his back flat against the trunk, staring at what he had done. Then he raised his head, and his eyes met mine.

I suppose it was natural that I did not seem able to move. I seemed to be in a trance.

I watched him draw out a pistol and take deliberate aim. I know his hand was unsteady, and I think the bullet went high; but the shot broke the spell that held me, and I heaved myself back down the bank before he could aim again.

I was on my feet in an instant, but, though I did not feel faint, I was shaking like a leaf. After a moment, however, I flung myself again at the bank, rather dazedly, but taking care to make the top at a different place.

Ellis was gone.

The body lay as it had fallen, and a big Alsatian was nosing and licking the face. Already there was a great stain upon the back of the light, tweed coat.

I leaped down lightly and, setting the dog aside, turned over the body as gently as I could. I remembered having read somewhere that you should not withdraw a knife. The man was breathing, so I carried him over and propped him against the bank. Then I ran for my flask, which was in the car. His eyes were half-open when I returned, and his hand was on the dog's collar, and the dog's head on his chest. I gave him what brandy I could, but most of it ran over his chin.

"I saw the whole thing," I said. "I'm sorry I couldn't warn you, but Ellis was too quick."

The other smiled faintly.

"But I'll get him," I added fiercely. "Tell me as much as you can."

The other shook his head.

"Let him go," he murmured. "Let him work out his own damnation. How much did you hear?"

"He wanted your secret," I said. "The Wagensburg treasure, you called it. And you didn't see the point."

He smiled again.

"Are you fond of dogs?" he breathed.

"Yes."

"Will you take care of mine?"

"I will."

He nodded.

"Good man," he whispered. Then, "Look in her collar," he murmured, "and you'll find she can pay for her keep."

His eyes closed then, and he lay so still for a while that I thought he was dead.

Suddenly –

"Raise me," he said. I did so. "What's England like?" he said. "I haven't been able to go there for seven years."

I tried to tell him.

"But the country's the same," he said thickly. "The woods, and the meadows at sundown and – "

That was his last word, for a terrible rush of blood came from his mouth, and he died as did Falstaff, speaking of green fields.

His blood was all over my hands and the dog's collar, but I presently found a stream and cleansed the two of us.

I had rather a business to keep the dog with me, for, though she was timid, she would have stayed with the corpse: but I turned a strap, which I had, into a leash and, speaking to her kindly, tried to show that I was her friend. And what with the excitement and horror of the whole business, my efforts to keep out of sight of passing vehicles, my constant outlook for Ellis and my anxiety to avoid association with the murder that had been done, I forgot to examine her collar for several hours. And this was as well, for my mind was full enough. Indeed, to this day, try as I will, I cannot tell how I came to Rouen nor yet to Dieppe. But I know that the car had been shipped and that I was aboard, arguing about quarantine, when I remembered the words of the dead Englishman.

In the same instant it came to me that, for such as had eyes to see, the collar was directly connecting me with the crime. As soon as convenient, therefore, I went up on deck, cut the leash down to a collar and, making the change in fear and trembling, stuffed the stout original into my coat pocket, out of which, do what I would, it bulged terribly.

Indeed more than once I came within an ace of dropping it overboard.

It was in my mind to say that I had found the dog collarless on the highway, and that was the tale I told at Newhaven as carelessly as I could. But, while I told it, I sweated, and the collar in my pocket felt like a packing-case.

It was late when I reached London, for there was no one at Newhaven who was licensed to receive the dog, and, though I might have left her in her hutch to await the coming of the carrier for whom I had sent, I had not the heart to do so. I have never seen a dumb animal, that was not bodily sick, in such evident distress. She would neither eat nor lie down, but sat for the most part with her head drooped, staring upon the ground. If ever I made to leave her, she would look at me so miserably that I spent the whole of the morning seated on a box by her side, and, when at length the carrier took her in charge, I could not meet her gaze, but, muttering some words of comfort, patted her hanging head and hurried away.

I drove straight to Brown's Hotel, there to find a letter from Hanbury asking me to dine that night at his father's house. I accepted immediately. Indeed, the invitation was just what I wanted, for I had already determined to tell Hanbury all that had happened to me the day before and to share with him whatever a scrutiny of the dog-collar might disclose.

And here I may say that I looked at the collar in my bedroom at Brown's Hotel, but could see nothing at all unusual within or without. The plate was engraved with a date, 17–10–16, which, I supposed, meant something to the dead man, but, except that it was un-English, there was nothing about it which called for any remark. I was sure, however, that when the leather was opened, we should find something within, and I hoped very much that this would prove of more interest than a hundred-pound note.

By the time I had bestowed the car and had bathed, it was six o'clock; so I put on evening clothes and, slipping the collar, which I had tied up with string so that it lay pretty flat, into my pocket, walked to the Club of which I had quite recently been elected a member.

It was unlikely that news of the murder would yet have reached England: for all that, I scanned every evening paper carefully; but there was nothing in any of them about the crime.

I was to dine at eight, but as soon as I had done with the papers, such was my impatience to see Hanbury that I felt I could wait no longer, and, very soon after seven, I went to the members' lobby where I had left my coat.

My coat was gone.

For a moment I stared blankly at the peg on which it had hung: then I began to go feverishly about the cloakroom, plucking at coat after coat which at all resembled mine and hoping desperately to come upon it.

I could only think that some member had made a mistake, for the Club was above suspicion and I could not believe that a stranger would have been so bold or so successful. Yet I was worried to death, because whoever had taken the coat was bound to find the collar and certain to remark the inscription upon the plate. Indeed, I saw myself going down to a very sea of troubles, for, you will remember, I had sworn I found the dog collarless, and thereby put myself on the wrong side of a matter the truth of which Ellis and I alone knew.

I had made my vain tour of the lobby and was standing there hot and helpless, wondering what I should do, when a tall, nice-looking man limped into the room.

I suppose my face told my story, for he looked straight at me and smiled.

"I'm awfully sorry," he said.

Then he slid out of his coat and held it for me to put on.

I stared like a fool.

"It's yours, isn't it?" he said. *"Dog-collar in the right-hand pocket?"*

"That's right," I blurted somehow.

Then I turned round and he helped me into the coat. "And a good thing too," he said. "But for that collar, I very much doubt if you'd ever have seen it again. It's exactly like mine. I didn't know there were two such good garments about. And this doesn't mean I'm not sorry, because I am. It was most careless of me."

I assured him that it did not matter and would have gone, but he detained me by talking, whilst he was finding his coat, and, when we went into the hall, he laid a hand on my shoulder and called a page.

"My name is Mansel," he said gravely. "I beg that you'll drink with me."

I found it difficult to refuse, so I said I would take a cocktail, and we went and stood by the fire and I told him my name.

When we had drunk, he turned.

"I must make a confession," he said. "I'm very interested in the date upon your dog-collar. Why did you put it there?"

There were a thousand answers: but I had not one upon my tongue. Yet, if I had been ready, I do not think I should have lied again. Honestly, I was rather grateful that the blow had fallen so soon, for, at least, in this way I had the chance of telling my tale before the papers told theirs, and Mansel had the look of a capable friend.

"I didn't put it there," said I.

"Ah," said he, and waited.

"I can't tell you now," I went on, "because it's too long a story, but if you'll make an appointment…"

"Any time after ten tonight," he said, and, with that, he gave me his card.

This bore the address of a flat in Cleveland Row.

"Can I bring a friend?" I said suddenly.

"Why certainly," said he.

We parted then, and I went to my dinner with George.

To him I said nothing, except that I had an engagement that night for both of us. He looked at me rather hard, but asked no questions, and at a quarter to ten we set out for Cleveland Row.

Looking back, it seems more than strange to me that upon such a little matter as a couple of similar overcoats, hung up upon neighbouring pegs, should have depended life and death and fortune. But so it fell out. For Jonathan Mansel was, I think, the only man in the world who could have captained our enterprise and brought it through such vicissitudes to a triumphant end.

Mansel and George Hanbury listened to my tale without a word.

When I had finished, Mansel sat back in his chair.

"I can't tell you much," he said. "But the inscription on that collar is not a date. It's a number. The man you saw murdered was in the secret service during the War. I knew him – as 'Number 171016.' He was known to be a crook but was a very good man. He'd a big future. Then Ellis cooked his goose – saddled him with four big robberies in open Court. They let him get out of the country, but of course he couldn't come back. He was broken up, I heard, for his heart was right in the game. I suppose that's why…"

He broke off and nodded at the collar.

For a while none of us spoke.

Then I took out a knife and passed it to Mansel.

"Will you open the collar?" I said.

We were sitting about a table, with the collar before us and a light hung above.

Mansel cut some stitches and, little by little, ripped the lining away. Almost at once some yellow material appeared, very stained and wrinkled and lying as flat against the collar as the lining itself. I made sure this was padding, but, when he had made the opening a little larger, Mansel got hold of the stuff and pulled it out.

It was a piece of oiled silk and seemed to have been part of a tobacco pouch, for, when it was unfolded, it had the form of an envelope without its flap. Within this again was a piece of thin notepaper, of which when it was opened, we could see three sides had been covered with a clear, close-written hand.

Mansel read it aloud, while Hanbury and I peered, one over either arm.

Statement of Carl Ramek, well-digger, aged 92.

My great-grandfather dug the great well of Wagensburg. He and his brother dug it with their father, the three working together in the great drought of 17—. The well is ninety feet deep. The first spring rises thirty feet down, so that normally there is sixty feet of water. There is no well like it hereabouts. They could not have got so deep but for the great drought. All the work in the well was done by my great-grandfather and his brother and their father alone. The masons cut the stones as they were told and brought them and the wood and the mortar to the top, but no one went down except the father and his two sons. That was by order of the Count. They used to sleep at the Castle, whilst they were doing this work. Out of the well there runs a shaft. The shaft leaves the well about eighty feet down. It runs up at an angle into a chamber. The chamber is just above the level of the first spring. No one knew of the shaft except my great-grandfather and his father and his brother and the Count. The shaft was very difficult to dig. The Count had an evil name and was very much feared. He would go down into the well to see the work. The rain came before the work was done, and the Count was beside himself for fear that they would not be able to finish it before the water came in. At the end they were working day and night. This was because the Count would let no one else go down the well. When the shaft and the chamber were done, the four of them went down one night when everyone else was asleep. The Count had two leather bags. These were very heavy. They got them down and up the shaft and into the chamber. It was raining hard, and the water was up to the shaft, and the next day it was above it. The three finished the masonry of the well, but the Count now allowed them helpers to keep the water down. On their last night at the Castle the Count killed two of the three with his own hands. My great-grandfather escaped, and though a long search was made for him, he was never found. He escaped into Italy and returned two years later, when the Count was dead. He always meant to go down and get the bags, but there was never another drought severe enough to empty the well. When he was dying he told my grandfather this and my grandfather told my father and he told me. I don't know which way the shaft runs. There are steps in the shaft. The Count cannot have recovered the bags because the great drought was followed by three very rainy years, and, as the springs are normally abundant, he could not have emptied the well without employing a lot of labour. I am unmarried and I have never told this to anyone else.

NOTE. The Count was clearly the notorious Axel the Red, who was nothing more or less than a common robber, and was reputed to have amassed a vast fortune. In 1760

Wagensburg was burnt and he perished in the flames. The castle passed to the Crown, and was sold twenty years later. It was then restored.

Wagensburg lies in Carinthia twenty-nine miles from Villach and four from Lerai.

September, 1904.

NOTE. W came into the market in 1904. Failed. Ellis knows.

June, 1910.

I stood and looked at George.

"Well," I said, "when do we start?"

George Hanbury shrugged his shoulders.

"Your time's mine," he said.

"And my time's Mansel's," said I.

I have often wondered how I came to say such a thing to a man upon whom, three hours before, I had never set eyes. Yet I meant what I said: and I think the truth is that the royalty of Mansel's nature had already subjected me, for I know that, if he had said at once that he could not join us, I should have been unreasonably dismayed.

Mansel rose from his chair and knocked out his pipe at the grate. Then he stood up quite straight and folded his hands.

"This may be a school-treat," he said, "and it may not. Treasure and trouble frequently go together. I haven't been Villach way since the year before the War, but unless things are very different to what they were – well, if you fought a duel with a couple of Lewis guns, nobody'd take the trouble to come and see what it was. As like as not they wouldn't hear you. It's not at all crowded. Well, that's all right for a school-treat." He stopped there for a moment. Then he proceeded thoughtfully. "Life's full of twists and turns, but to take on a job like this is to tackle Blind Corner itself; and it's never policed. Whether you two are free to go is your affair. I will go – upon one condition, which I see slight reason why you should accept. The condition

13

is that from first to last in this venture you two will do what I say. You see, I'm older."

I thought the condition a very mild one and said as much; so did Hanbury. But it has occurred to me since that I should have found it presumptuous in anyone else.

Be that as it may, we gave our words to obey him in every particular, and then we sat down at his feet while he rough-hewed our campaign.

Of this, he showed that there would be three phases. First, the acquisition of Wagensburg; then, the lifting of the treasure; and, lastly, the disposal of it. And, since all he said was very much to the point, I will use, so far as I can recall them, his very words.

"The first thing to do is to buy the property. Until we're the landlords, the treasure is not ours to lift. To rent the place may be simpler and, so, tempting; but I don't see the force of finding a King's ransom for somebody else. If Wagensburg's in the market, well and good. I'll find the money; I don't think the price will be high. If it's not in the market, we shall have to pay more than it's worth; but in these days you can usually buy a place even if it's not for sale.

"To get to the treasure shouldn't be difficult, but, unless the well's dry, I'm sure we can't do it alone. To keep pace with springs that give freely is very hard work; it's a very deep well; all wells are dangerous. We may even find that we can't use the well at all, but must drive a new shaft from above. Above all, it's most important that we should not be disturbed. We should only have to be seen at work to be suspected. To my way of thinking, it's at least a six-man job. If we each take a servant who's honest and fit and game, we shall get there quicker and better and much more comfortably.

"How we shall dispose of the treasure is a matter we can only decide when we see what shape it takes.

"So much for the plan of action.

"What turns the whole thing from an exercise into a venture is the fact that *Ellis knows*. Whether we shall clash with him or not, we can't possibly tell. I hardly think it's likely myself. Sooner or later, of course, Wagensburg will draw Ellis as a magnet draws steel. 'Where your treasure is,' you know. But, when a man's just done a murder, he usually lies pretty low; and, when he knows that somebody saw him do it, he lies lower still. For all that, what Ellis will not understand is why you haven't gone to the police. That will make him think very hard. And, knowing that you overheard what the dead man said, he may attribute your silence to a wish to hide something which reference to the police would disclose. In which case we should clash... Because of this possibility we've got to move on our toes, always go the long way round and watch with both eyes. Remember this. Whether he knows it or not, we're going to get in Ellis' way. He may never know it. But if he does know it, well, you've seen what he does with people who get in his way – provided they give him the chance."

That was as much as he said at that time; while I saw the force of most of it, I did not agree that there was anything to fear from Ellis, for, though, as I had reason to know, he was a desperate man, I could not believe that he would challenge six men at once and I was quite certain that if and when he did he would lose his match.

Then we found pencil and paper and, taking the well-digger's statement, made a plan of the well and did what we could to "place" the chamber.

We were all agreed that it would be pleasanter to reach the chamber by digging than by way of the well. The shaft had been mostly full of water for some hundred and sixty years: the chamber had been sealed for the same period: and, if you must visit places so long abandoned to Nature, it is very much more agreeable to have the daylight at your back. But, though the prospect of inspecting them by lantern was not inviting, it was,

I think, the unmistakable likeness which the plan bore to a trap that made us strive so hard to find out another way.

But we could not.

Without knowing the angle at which the shaft had been driven and the direction in which it left the well, we could make out no more than that the roof of the chamber must lie about twenty-five feet below the ground and would most likely be encountered not more than twenty and not less than ten paces from the side of the well. This did not sound so formidable to Mansel and me, but, after a great deal of labour, George, who alone of us laid any claim to mathematical powers, demonstrated to our amazement that even that would leave some eight hundred square yards to be searched, and we gave up the attempt.

We studied the statement and the plan we had made until we knew them by heart, and we raked the former for inferences, until we had almost deduced the proportions of the Count; but it was not an unprofitable enterprise, for, by the time we had done, it was plain that, when we went abroad, statement and plan could both be left with some Bank, because, short of loss of reason, nothing could ever erase their particulars from our minds.

Then we discussed preparations and how soon we could start, and the getting of the servants, and what my uncle would say when told I was going to travel during the summer months. But we always came back to the treasure and the chamber and the great well.

It was two o'clock in the morning before Mansel sent us away, bidding us do nothing but get some serviceable clothes and hold our tongues.

Unless he summoned us, we were not to see him for a week, but then we were to dine with him in Cleveland Row. If all had gone well, he said, he saw no reason why we should not start a week from that day.

"One thing more," he added, as we stood in his hall. "The dog or the collar may link you up with the crime. I think it unlikely. But at the first breath of trouble come straight to me."

I need no such instruction. Mansel had become the pillar of my state.

Indeed I had made up my mind to seek him the moment I found anywhere a report of the murder. But, though each day I searched the papers faithfully, there was no mention made of it.

Nor was there at any time, so far as I saw. I never read the French papers, but I often doubt that the murder was reported at all. The venue was lonely; the victim was foreign and had probably few friends; and, if no great search was made, the body may well have escaped notice, until there was little for an unpractised eye to find irregular.

The next day I visited the dog and found her in good hands. The home to which she had been taken was a famous establishment, with special quarters for dogs in quarantine, and from the condition and spirits of the many dogs I saw it was plain that everything possible was done to lighten their confinement.

The poor animal was delighted to see me, and, observing her pleasure, the kennel-man was quick to bring her some fresh food in the hope that she would now break the fast she had stubbornly maintained. To our relief she did so and soon left her plate clean, and though, when I went away, she made frantic endeavours to follow, the man insisted that she would pine no longer and that, when next I came, I should find her a different dog.

I am glad to say this came true: and, by the time I left England, she was eating regularly and seemed contented with her lot.

To my surprise, the interview I had with my uncle passed off smoothly enough. He certainly gave me no blessing, but, beyond remarking that six months in the City of London were of more value than twice that time spent "knocking about"

Europe, he made little protest against the postponement of my apprenticeship. He then sat down and wrote me out a cheque for three hundred pounds, and, when I stammered my thanks, he said very gravely that that was a present for "singeing the King of Spain's beard." At first I could not think of what he meant, but I afterwards realized that I owed money and favour to my discomfiture of the communists, whose doctrines and practices he held in great abhorrence.

The week of inaction to which Mansel had committed Hanbury and myself passed very slowly, and there were moments when we felt almost mutinous. But, when we began to discuss the preparations which we should have been making, if Mansel had not told us to hold our hands, the wisdom of his order became immediately plain, for we were soon out of our depth and invariably quarrelled over the very vulnerable plans we laid, till the only matter upon which we were entirely agreed was the vanity of each other's proposals.

On the last day but one, however, a note from Mansel came to salve my impatience. In this he said that he had found a man whom he thought I might like to be my servant, that the latter would call upon me at ten on the following day and that I was to examine him thoroughly from every point of view *for*, the letter concluded, *although I will answer for his past, he is particularly to serve you and you will be responsible for his engagement.*

I soon found that Hanbury had received a similar note, and this real evidence of progress excited us out of all reason. At the same time we were both a little uneasy at the thought of taking a decision which, if it proved mistaken, might be the undoing of us all. Of any man who was admitted to our secret would be required a discretion and loyalty which were today uncommon and might easily be called upon to bear an extraordinary strain. To recognize these qualities in repose demanded an insight which we knew very well indeed we did not possess. To add to our concern, we did not know what Mansel had told the candidates and whether we ought to disclose that the service they were ready to enter was no ordinary one. In the end we sent him a note, asking for directions, but, though he received it, he sent no answer at all, but only, as he afterwards told us, pitched it into the fire.

We had, therefore, to use our own judgement as best we could, but that we engaged Bell and Rowley and that they turned out so well cannot be counted to our credit, for I think an idiot could have seen the stuff of which they were made.

Bell was my servant. He was a quiet, little man, very sturdily built. He was serious and well-spoken, but, though he was respectful, he had none of the manner of a servant and looked like a countryman turned clerk, which I afterwards found he was. He seemed to notice nothing, yet was exceptionally observant, and he always wore the same agreeable, but something resigned expression, as though his face were a mask. I never knew him volunteer a statement unless he thought it might be of service: he never once complained: he was most faithful, and I think he thought Mansel was a god. In this tenet he was not peculiar. Rowley and Carson, Mansel's servant, held the same view.

I shall ever remember our dinner with Mansel, if for no other reason, because it is the solitary occasion upon which expectations which I knew it was foolish to harbour have been so startlingly exceeded.

He gave us a short dinner, which was very well cooked and served, and we drank a pink champagne, which I believe was a very rare wine though I fear that neither Hanbury nor I was old enough to appreciate its quality, but only the fact that Mansel was doing us honour. Throughout the meal our venture was not mentioned, except that he said he was glad that we liked the men he had sent, and we talked for the most part of Oxford, "which," he said, "is the only place in the world where a man may eat his cake and have it too, for the years he wastes there are beyond measure profitable."

It was after the cloth had been drawn and the servants had left the room that he told us quietly that all had "panned out" very well, and that, if we had no objection, we would start in two days' time. Before we had recovered from our astonishment, he began to relate exactly what he had done, wasting no words and in no way pretending to authority, but, when they were not apparent, giving his reasons for his actions and speaking as though he were a staff-officer reporting to his equal or senior the measures which he had taken in accordance with orders received. The manifest excellence of his forethought apart, how he had accomplished so much was a sheer mystery to me and ever will be, for I never in my life saw him hurry or use the telephone, and he had spent the weekend in Hampshire, as he always did when living at Cleveland Row.

Be that as it may, our preparations were complete, and we were to start on Thursday, that is, in two days' time.

I will not set down his tale of the arrangements he had made, because they will presently appear, but will only say that the servants were to take our baggage to a hotel at Salzburg, that we were to travel to the same town by car, and that such as might desire to know our business were told that Mansel was a great trout fisherman and that we were all three bound for the streams of Carinthia to see what could be done in that quarter.

And here I may say that anyone who was told this was shown one side of the truth, for Mansel was more fond of fishing than of almost anything else, and Hanbury and I learned our first lessons in the art of angling not very far from Wagensburg itself.

That his preparations had involved a certain outlay was clear, but, when we spoke of money and stammeringly asked to be allowed to contribute towards the expense, Mansel said that such matters could wait until the treasure was found: however, on our persisting, he promised to keep an account and to consider two-thirds of all that he was expending as our affair.

Then we gave him our passports, for he was to look them over and have them ordered to his liking.

After that he brought out the well-digger's statement and the map we had made, and, when we had studied them both for as long as we pleased, he sealed them up in an envelope and asked me the name of my Bank. I told him. Then he wrote upon the envelope:

171016. This is the property of Richard William Chandos, and is lodged for safe custody with the Manager of the Pall Mall Branch of —'s Bank.

and gave it to me.

"You must lodge that tomorrow," he said, "and see that you get a receipt."

This I promised to do.

Then, of course, we fell to talking of our venture, but, after telling us something of the country in the heart of which Wagensburg lay – for, though he did not know the castle, he had stayed in those parts for one summer before the War – Mansel began to speak of trout and trout-fishing and very soon had us engrossed in what he said, which, I think, was just what he wanted, for, if we were to set up for fishermen, it was as well that we should know something of the art. And from trout he led us to streams, and from streams to rivers, and thence, naturally, again to Oxford, and there we stayed very contentedly until it was time for us to go.

At ten on Thursday morning we were to meet again – an engagement which Hanbury and I would not have missed or exchanged for one of the very bags which the Count had borne down the well, for there we were to get into Mansel's Rolls-Royce and drive with him to Dover and so, by France and Germany, clean into Carinthia.

21

Yet, as it happened, we did not keep that engagement, and the plans which Mansel had laid were unfulfilled; and the whole face of our adventure was changed in the twinkling of an eye, before it was ever begun. And all this, because I stopped in the street to look into a window.

2

The Way to Wagensburg

It was the next morning when I was walking down St James's Street on my way to the Bank, that I stopped to glance at the maps which were spread in a shop window. I had done so many times before, for I often went by that way and, though I am no geographer, a map or a plan has for me some attraction to which I invariably yield. I had taken my look and was just about to pass on when I suddenly observed before me a map of Southern Austria, drawn to a large scale.

I was naturally most interested and at once began to look for Wagensburg, for so large was the scale that the property might well have been marked: but, though I soon saw Villach, most of the names were not at all easy to read, for the country was plainly very mountainous and the lettering was often lost against the heavy shading of the heights. For all that, if I could have gone closer I think I might soon have found the name I was seeking, but the map was some way from the glass, and I could not even stand fairly in front of it, because of another idler, who was standing before the window, regarding its wares. I waited a moment or two, expecting that he would pass on, but he did not, so I approached my face as close to the pane as I could without flattening my nose, in one last endeavour to locate the castle before I gave up the attempt. At this, the other seemed to notice my presence and turned to look at me, and, when instinctively I glanced at him, I saw that it was Ellis himself.

I do not know which of us was the more taken aback, but Ellis was the first to recover and turn away. For myself, I stood gaping and staring after him, as he walked rather jerkily away towards Piccadilly.

My first impulse was to follow him, though what good that would have done I do not know: and indeed I started uncertainly to hasten up the street in his wake; but what design I had was soon frustrated, for he entered a cab which was crawling close to the kerb and was instantly driven away.

I have often wondered what would have been his feelings if he had known of the statement which lay in my breast-pocket, while we were shoulder to shoulder before the window, and whether he would not have made some desperate attempt to possess himself of the document there and then; and, all things considered, I verily believe he would have tried, for, because of that paper, he had already put his neck in a noose, and, as the saying is, a man may "as well be hanged for a sheep as a lamb."

The disappearance of Ellis must have restored my wits, for I realized in a flash that the first thing which I must do was to inform Mansel. I, therefore, ran down the street to Cleveland Row and happily found him in the act of leaving his flat.

Directly he saw me, he turned, and I followed him through his hall and into the dining-room.

"Yes?" he said shortly.

I told my tale, and he frowned.

"I don't know whether this is good luck or bad," he said. "But I think it's bad luck. Anyway we must take no chances." He thought for a moment there. Then he went on: "Ellis now knows for certain that Wagensburg interests you. If your excitement was apparent, he may even suspect that you hold the secret itself. That you made no attempt to detain him wouldn't weigh much with me, because a good many people would hesitate to seize a man in the West End for a murder which nobody knows has been committed in France; but he would probably ascribe your failure to reluctance to court inquiry. So I'm glad you followed him."

"I expect the cab had a back window," said Mansel. "Any way, Ellis will act. He may even try to watch." He took out his case and lighted a cigarette. "I'd like you and Hanbury to take the boat-train tomorrow. And I'll go over tonight."

Then he gave me careful directions, told me on no account to return to Cleveland Row and not to walk alone after dark.

"You see," he said, "you've lost Ellis, but you mustn't make sure that Ellis has lost you. I rather expect he's thinking of other things, but you never can tell. And those cabs can turn on sixpence."

As I walked down Pall Mall, I felt as though every step I took was marked by a hundred eyes.

I lodged the envelope at the Bank, and then drove off to find Hanbury and tell him of the change in our plans. Then we went out together and bought two tickets to Paris for the following day.

I do not suppose two men ever used their eyes as we did from then until we saw Mansel again; and that, I imagine, was just what Mansel wanted, for, although I do not think he thought it likely that I should be followed, he would have been very glad to know what Ellis was doing and whether the man was alone or going to work with a gang. But Hanbury and I proved broken reeds, and, when we rejoined him, we had nothing at all to report; and this shows of how much use we were, for it afterwards appeared that Ellis had turned at the top of St James's Street and had driven back to see me turn into Cleveland Row, that I had been followed to the Bank, to Hanbury's father's house and to Cook's office, and that it was

25

only at Boulogne that touch with me had been lost. And for that relief we had Mansel's prevision to thank.

At four that afternoon the commissionaire attached to my Club brought me my passport and took away all my luggage, both light and heavy; and, when I left Town the next morning, the suitcase I took with me held nothing but worn-out clothes, for which I had no use. Of Hanbury the same can be said. We left by the morning train, and came to Boulogne about noon of a beautiful day. We were soon off the boat and, since we had reserved no seats in the Paris train, we made a fuss of securing the ones we wanted as well as a table for the first luncheon to be served. When our luggage was up on the rack and the porters had been dismissed, we strolled up and down the platform, like everyone else, but, after a little, we wandered on to the quay and presently out of sight.

We made our way to a tavern in the heart of the town, and there found Mansel's Rolls-Royce, and, within, Mansel himself, smoking and drinking beer, and arguing with the host about the Battle of the Somme. He had come that day from Dieppe.

He seemed very pleased to see us, and ordered luncheon at once, "for," said he, "I want to be in Strasbourg by dawn, and lie up there for the day. I was watched out of London last night, and, though they've lost me now, they'll probably make a fresh cast."

"But what could they do," said Hanbury, "if they pick you up on the road?"

"Why, what they have done," said Mansel, "not very far from Chartres. Don't forget," he added, "that we three hold the secret which that man held. And I think Ellis thinks we do."

And there, I think, for the first time, it came to me how great was the power of those two leather bags which lay in the chamber of the great well, and I seemed to see them as impassive, relentless twin gods, bringing this man to death and holding that man for the gallows and sending another four or

26

five pelting across a continent, like so many thieves in the night, to God knows what fortune, while, as for the hatred and malice and uncharitableness which they were inspiring, even the compilers of the Litany cannot have contemplated so poisonous a flow of soul. But, though it seemed very shocking, I felt very cheerful to think I was one of the "thieves," and the thought of stealing a march upon men so bold and determined as Ellis and his friends, was like a glass of champagne.

Whilst we were lunching, a basket was stocked with provisions against our journey and then tied up in two cloths because of the dust. Indeed, great attention was paid us by the people of the inn, who manifestly knew Mansel and thought the world of him.

We all ate very well, while Mansel spoke of the car. Of this he was plainly proud, and I was surprised that he thought it wise to leave her alone in the street. I said so presently, when he laughed and asked me to fetch him a map which he had left on its seat. I went to do so and found the car guarded better than I had dreamed. As I leaned over the side, a small, white dog rose from the driver's place, and, had I been the devil himself, I could not have been accorded a more hostile reception. The whole street rang with a storm of barking, and if I had taken the map, I should certainly have paid in blood for my capture. At this, Mansel appeared and, after making much of the terrier, a pure-bred Sealyham, picked him up out of the car and put him into my arms. I stroked and spoke to him, and presently he licked my face.

"And now," said Mansel, "he knows that you are my friend and will let you come and go and do as you please."

Then he called Hanbury and made him free of the dog's confidence in the same way. After that, he asked me, if I had done eating, to stay in the car, because he wanted to give the Sealyham his lunch; for he set great store by the terrier, as was very proper, for I never saw a more attractive or intelligent dog.

His name was Tester, and I believe, so fine was his instinct, that he understood every word that was said to him and many that were not; and I know that from that time on I was his most obedient servant, and he my very good friend; but more than that he never was, for Mansel was his master, and he knew no other.

The car was a new model, and the coachwork had been carefully done. It was, as Mansel said, a true "touring" body, for though it was slim to look at, it had great capacity and was so constructed that two could sleep in it with ease and comfort, and, when it appeared to be empty, its hidden lockers concealed all manner of stuff not usually carried in cars, but invaluable to a pioneer. There were brandy and "first field dressings," a medicine-chest and bandages, lint and splints; but most important in my eyes was a little armoury of weapons and ammunition and handcuffs, "of which," said Mansel, "I hope we shall have no need; but I like to think that they're there." Then he showed us that in the driver's pocket he carried a heavy pistol, ready for use; and that, I think, completed my conviction that Ellis was trying to play a losing game and would very soon curse Wagensburg and the day he first heard its name.

It was half past two when we left Boulogne for Strasbourg, and a wonderful journey it was. I sat with Mansel and Tester, and Hanbury sat behind. It had been raining a little, but was now very fine; the country through which we passed was agreeably fresh and blowing; and the car had the way of a swallow in the air. Mansel drove very fast, without seeming to do so, and maintained an average of forty-five to the hour with astonishing precision. He neither hurried through towns nor showed any inconsideration to man or beast upon the road, but such time as he lost on this account he won when the road was open without any fuss, for the car was willing, and he was a remarkable judge of pace and distance, and, while he was yet a great way from some predicament, could tell to a hair what was within his power; and that is more than most men can do.

When evening came and we began to see cows being driven home, we turned down a lane and stopped. Then Mansel and Hanbury alighted and took Tester for a stroll, whilst I stayed with the car and prepared our supper. This we ate easily, for we were to stay there an hour. Except to take in petrol, we did not stop again till we came to Strasbourg; and that was at one o'clock. There was a fine moon, and I remember looking up sleepily to see how the old cathedral was lacking one of its spires. We chose a small hotel in an unimportant street, and only two rooms were taken, for Mansel slept in the car in a garden at the back of the inn.

We had reached Strasbourg sooner than Mansel had expected, and, though he had intended to stay in that city till dusk, the thought of wasting the whole of a valuable day was more than he could endure, and by nine o'clock of that morning we were again upon the road.

Our way now lay through the Black Forest and was at times most solitary. Mansel drove with his ears pricked, and if ever I spoke, begged me to hold my tongue; but I could not share his vigilance and, when we stopped for a moment by the side of the way, asked him how Ellis could have had time to contrive our pursuit or attack.

His reply was unanswerable.

"I could have done it," he said, "with luck and money and friends, and, though the first can't be bought, the other two can. Ellis had a secret to sell. Be sure he's sold it, for he couldn't fight us alone. Therefore, he has money and friends. And, since the Castle of Wagensburg is plainly everyone's way, not to look out for us would be the act of a fool. They know that we're going direct, because we've no time to spare. That suggests Strasbourg. So somebody flies to Paris and gets to Strasbourg some hours ahead of us. They can't watch a city, but they can watch the frontier posts. And, don't forget, *buried treasure* is the very deuce of a goad."

As he spoke, a very faint sound came to our ears.

It was the high-pitched note of a powerful electric horn, as yet some distance away and between us and Strasbourg.

Mansel had the Rolls moving before I was well in my seat, and we were very soon doing some sixty odd miles to the hour, but the next time I heard the horn it sounded much closer, and, after a moment, Mansel slackened his speed and let a closed car go by. He was very careful, however, to keep this in sight, and when, two or three miles on, we saw it slow down and stop in the middle of the road, he asked me to fasten Tester to a short chain which was attached to the coachwork close to my feet.

As we approached, a man who had alighted from the car spread out his arms as a signal to us to stop, not in a peremptory manner, but rather as does a man who is in need of assistance. Mansel waved in reply and applied his brakes, but he overran the closed car by nearly a hundred yards, before bringing the Rolls to rest on the crown of the road.

Then we turned round in our seats and waited for the stranger to move.

For a while he seemed to be expecting that we should come back, but, when it was quite evident that we were not going to move, he spoke for a moment with someone within the car and then began to walk in our direction.

"Hanbury," said Mansel quietly, "watch that car. The moment it moves, ask Chandos to give you a match."

The stranger was wearing dark glasses, which he did not remove; his hair was fair and his complexion ruddy. He was not very tall, and his hands were coarse and rough. He walked jauntily and wore his hat on one side.

As he came up, he gave us "Good day" in French, and then very haltingly inquired if any one of us could speak English.

"We are English," said Mansel.

"Why, that's fine," said the other. Then very calmly he asked us to come back and look at his car, "for," said he, "she seems to be nearly red-hot, and none of us knows enough to change a wheel."

"If she's so hot," said Mansel, "no one can help you at all for half an hour. I should open both sides of the bonnet and push her into the shade. I'll send you help from the very next garage I pass."

"Now be a sport," said the stranger, laying a hand on the Rolls and casually lifting his hat. "Come an' 'ave a look at the swine."

"Bill," said Hanbury to me, "give me a match."

"Shall I send you help?" said Mansel, as the Rolls began to move.

The stranger's answer was to try to apply the handbrake, but, as he was feeling for the lever, I hit him under the jaw, and he fell back into the road.

Then the Rolls shot forward, and, as I was unready, I fell myself upon Mansel, who was laughing like a child at a circus, while Tester was barking uproariously and trying to burst his chain, and Hanbury was kneeling on the back seat, shouting "Gone away" and making derisive gestures with both hands.

Before I had got my balance, the closed car was out of sight, but Hanbury told us, with tears, that its occupants' haste to alight, before it had stopped, had done as much damage as I, for that, as a man was descending from the front of the car, someone behind him flung open the second door and that this hit the one in the back and knocked him down and then returned upon the other, who was himself half-way out. So it seemed that we had had very much the best of the brush and that Ellis and his friends had gained nothing but a couple of heavy falls; but Mansel, when he had done laughing, began to frown, "because," said he, "though I'd sooner be before than behind them, I'd very much sooner not be on their road at all. Too many circumstances over which one has no control, on the road today."

The words were hardly out of his mouth, when we rounded a bend to see a level-crossing ahead. And the barriers were down.

When we were very near, Mansel stopped and Hanbury and I leaped out. At once, as there was no keeper, we endeavoured to raise the poles, but these had been lowered by machinery, controlled, I suppose, by some distant signalman, and were fast locked into place.

"Never mind," said Mansel quietly, stepping out of the driver's seat. "Chandos, you take my place, and, Hanbury, sit by his side."

With that, he climbed into the back and lighted a cigarette.

We did as he said, and, the engine running, I sat with my hand on the lever and my foot on the clutch wondering what was to happen and reflecting rather dismally that we had laughed too soon.

It was a quiet place, and the sunshine was very hot. Except for the murmur of the engine, there was no sound at all.

So we sat, waiting for the train or the closed car.

Two minutes must have gone by before the latter appeared, rounding the bend like fury and raising a storm of dust.

"Don't start till I say so," said Mansel, and slewed himself round on the seat.

The road was none too wide, and we were full on the crown.

With my eyes on the driving mirror, I saw the car approach.

It was in the driver's mind to thrust alongside, but, if he had done so, he could not have crossed the metals, for the gate was less wide than the road; so he brought his car to rest behind us and a little to the right.

"If anyone moves," said Mansel, "I'm going to fire." The windows of the car were open, so they heard what he said.

"You've tried to stop me by force and you've pursued me; and at the first town I come to I'm going to prefer a charge. My papers are all in order; I've a licence to carry a pistol; and my luggage is in the car. Perhaps you can say the same. If you can't, you'll be detained – pending inquiries."

"Bluff," said someone.

"Then call it," said Mansel.

"You've assaulted us," said another. "I asked you a civil question, an' you slogged me under the jaw. An' you talk about the police."

"Yes," said Mansel, "I do. Because my record's clean. Then again, I speak German quite well; and that's a great help."

"Bluff," said the first speaker. "You know as well as I do that you won't go to the police. You can't afford to."

"If you mean," said Mansel, "that I don't want to waste my time, that's perfectly true."

"I don't," said the other. "I meant that, much as you like 'em, the last thing you want just now is to catch the eye of the police."

Mansel raised his eyebrows.

"I'm not going to argue," he said, "but I can't help thinking that you're mistaking me for somebody else. Excuse me," and, with that, he fired.

The silence which succeeded the explosion was that of the grave. I had, of course, jumped violently and now sat still in my seat, as if under a spell, though my heart was pounding like a labouring pump and I was expecting every instant the shock of battle. But this did not come. So far as I could see by the mirror, those in the closed car were sitting as still as I, and, after a moment or two, Mansel spoke again.

"The next time anyone moves, I shall try to hit him," he said. "And I think perhaps it would be better if you all four folded your arms. Thank you."

"Today to you," said the man who had spoken last.

"Indubitably," said Mansel.

Then we were left to our thoughts, and to wonder if ever the train was coming by.

I was disquieted.

Mansel had spoken boldly, but you cannot make bricks without straw, and the man who had taken him up was not even shaken, very much less deceived. For the moment we had them in check, but the changes and chances of the road were manifold, and, unless we could run right away, as like as not we should be cornered again. And the next time they would be more careful.

It was while I was thinking of these things that I happened to lower my eyes to the mat at my feet, and there, beneath me, I saw an adjustable spanner. Mansel had used it that morning to tighten a bolt, and, in his haste, had omitted to put it away.

Shakespeare had said somewhere that "the sight of means to do ill deeds, Makes deeds ill done." So it was with the spanner. For directly I saw it, I thought that here was the means to spoil the petrol-tank of the closed car and so put the enemy out of action.

I picked up the spanner, slid this into my pocket and turned to Hanbury.

"Take my place," I said quietly. "I'm going to disable their car."

Hanbury blinked once or twice and gulped as though he would protest, so soon as he found his tongue; but I opened my door and stepped out without more ado.

I sauntered up to the barrier and glanced up and down the rails. Then I turned round and looked at the two cars.

Hanbury was in my place and Mansel did not seem to have moved. He was sitting easily sideways, covering the car with his pistol and supporting his right wrist with his left arm. The four men, of whom Ellis was not one, were wearing blue glasses and sitting like images, with folded arms.

I stepped to the radiator of the Rolls, unscrewed the cap and peered within. Then I frowned and, spanner plainly in hand, stooped as though to tighten the plug. After appearing and disappearing once or twice, I replaced the cap, still frowning, and disappeared again. A moment later I was beneath the car. It was a tight fit, but the pulse of the closed car's engine covered the noise I made. I worked along on my back as best I could, until my head was level with the Rolls' hind wheels. To pass from beneath the Rolls to beneath the closed car meant crossing about six feet of open road, but there was not more than a yard between the two cars' wings, and, though, from where I lay, I could see the hat of the man beside the driver, I judged that, unless he moved, the strip of road I must pass was just out of his sight. So, since to see where I was going was now essential, I turned very gently upon my face and took a deep breath. Inch by inch I covered those six feet of open road, and I must admit that I did it with my heart in my mouth, for I could by no means be sure that I was not in some view, and, though I hoped for the best, once one of the enemy knew that I was beneath their car, pistol or no, it was most unlikely that they would make no attempt to learn my business.

At last, however, it was over, and I was well out of sight and under the closed car.

I turned again upon my back, and there I lay for a moment to get my breath, for the strain of moving so flat upon my face had been exhausting, and the heat and noise of the engine at such close quarters had been unpleasant. I was, too, half choked and blinded with the dust, which hereabouts lay very thick.

As I was taking my rest, I became suddenly aware of a great noise, which was not that of the engine, but seemed to be coming upon me at a terrible speed. For an instant I lay paralysed, unable to think what it was. Then, in a flash, I knew it was the sound of the train for which we had waited so long.

What would happen when it had gone by and the barriers rose, I did not stay to think. Indeed, I do not remember how I got to the tank, but I know that I was fumbling with the spanner and that the dust was falling thick into my mouth and eyes as the train roared on its way.

The bottom of the tank was all encrusted with dirt, but I had this off in a twinkling and fitted the spanner to the plug. Twice I tried to move it, and twice it refused to budge, for I do not think it had ever been undone since the car was built, but had been painted over, so that its shape was half gone and it might not have been a plug at all, but only a knob.

I had just reset the spanner, licked my hands and taken another hold, when a sudden, unmistakable clatter announced that the barriers were up.

At once I heard Mansel's voice.

"Stand by, William," he said, using my Christian name. And then: "I'm going now," he continued, "to prefer my charge. From what you say I gather you're going to follow, so we shall meet again."

He said more, but that was as much as I heard, for his words showed me something I had not dreamed of, namely, that *he did not know that I was not still in the Rolls*, but thought he was free to proceed, and – what was perhaps more serious – that upon this important point the four in the closed car were better informed than he.

With these thoughts in my mind, I put forth all my strength, and I think any screw must have yielded to the frantic effort I made. The drain-plug gave way with a crack, and, after one or two turns, I felt the petrol running over my hands. I continued to work desperately, and, a moment later the plug fell out of its hole, and, with a soft gush, the spirit began to pour out into the dust.

I thrust the drain-plug into my pocket, because, without that, a hogshead of petrol would not avail the closed car, but she would have to be towed until she came to some place which boasted a lathe and a man sufficiently skilled to fashion a substitute. Then, regardless of the downpour of petrol, I scrambled clear of the car. As I did so, I heard Mansel raise his voice.

"William," he cried, "don't look for it any more: we must have dropped it farther back."

I knew at once that Hanbury must have told him my errand, and that now he was giving me my cue: so, wondering how the inmates of the closed car would take my appearance, I stepped to the middle of the road, and then, waving the spanner, jogged cheerfully into view.

As I came alongside: "Let her go," said Mansel.

Hanbury had set the door open, and the car was moving when I flung myself in. As the Rolls swept over the metals, I heard a shout of surprise, and this was immediately followed by a veritable bellow of rage, which I like to think showed that the occupants of the closed car accredited me with some malicious attempt upon its efficiency. And I think that in that I am right, for instead of pursuing, they all flung out of the car, and, when we sailed round a bend, they were behind their vehicle, which was standing apparently deserted, with all four doors open, to the side of the dusty road.

Then Mansel took over the wheel, and I showed him and Hanbury the drain-plug and told my tale. Presently we ran through a village, where there was not so much as a forge, and a few miles further on we came to a smooth-flowing stream. Here Mansel gave me five minutes to strip and bathe, and, while I did so, Hanbury unpacked clean clothes for me to put on. When I came back to the car, they had opened three bottles of beer and drank my health in the most handsome fashion. But I think it is clear that, though anyone, who was not too fat, could have crawled underneath the two cars, only a great personality could have held four such villains at bay for nearly ten minutes and so brought us safe and sound out of so perilous a pass.

We came to Salzburg that night, to find the three servants arrived and our rooms waiting; and here Mansel slept in a bed for the first time since he had left London, while Carson, his servant, lay in the car in his stead.

The next day we breakfasted together in Hanbury's room, and there, after we had eaten, a council was held.

It was most probable that, if Wagensburg was in the market, some one of the agents in Salzburg had the castle upon his books; and, since Ellis had taken the field, at once to set about the purchase seemed plainly the best thing to do. Yet, to seek to buy property of such consequence without having so much as seen it, was out of the question, for not only should we be unable to judge the price we were asked, but such an astonishing action would be certain to arouse comment: and that was the last thing we desired.

We, therefore, determined to devote the next day to a reconnaissance, in the course of which we should explore the country round Wagensburg, and, if it was vacant, the property itself. We should then, at least, be qualified to play the part of people so much attracted by a domain as to desire to own it, and, though an agent might think we had more money than brains, it was unlikely that he would look for any deeper explanation of our eagerness.

Another thing we decided was to purchase a second car. Sooner or later we must have one, for the Rolls would not hold six as well as baggage, and it might well prove worse than inconvenient to break our party in two. And, since to carry out the reconnaissance in some car less distinctive than the Rolls might be to our advantage, we determined to make our purchase before we did anything else.

Then Mansel requested Hanbury to stay in Salzburg, while he and I and Carson went out alone. It was a big thing to ask, but Hanbury immediately agreed in the most handsome way, insisting that he would be better employed in caring for the Rolls after her long run than in making a fourth in what was "a three-men job." But Mansel made him promise not to go out alone, but always to take with him one of the other servants, when he left the hotel.

By midday we had a car. It was not new, but had been carefully used, and had only come to be sold the day before. It bore a well-known name, was swift and very well found, and, after putting it to several tests, Mansel drove to a Bank and paid the price we were asked without more ado.

Then we ate a short luncheon, bade Hanbury goodbye, and, taking Carson and Tester, left for Carinthia soon after one o'clock.

It was a notable run. The country was mountainous, and the scenery superb; the further South we went the more picturesque became the way, and the villages grew less frequent and more and more unspoiled.

Everywhere there were woods and forests, high and low, and, among them, streams and pastures and an occasional farm, with a saucer on every ridge-pole to keep the witches away.

About sundown we came to a village that Mansel knew.

There was but one inn, and that did not look as if it had much to offer, although, to judge by its size and style, it must once have been a house of some importance and have served people of quality. But, as it turned out, I was never better lodged in my life; for I slept in a great four-poster amid furniture which must have been of great value; my huge room was spotless; the linen was unusually fine and smelt very sweet of some herbs, with which it had been laid away; and the attendance was such as, I imagine, travellers used to hope for a hundred years ago. The fare, too, was excellent – trout, and an omelet and most delicious bread, with plenty of fresh fruit and cream; and, since there was no garage or coach-house, they opened the great doors that belonged to the house itself, and Mansel drove the car into a vast, flagged hall, to the great entertainment of the regular customers of the inn, who were there gathered drinking, before they went to their beds.

We were on the road the next morning by six o'clock, and before it was seven we had sighted Wagensburg.

We had stopped for a moment by the way to study the map, and I was trying to determine exactly which road we were using, when Mansel gave a light laugh and touched me upon the arm.

I followed his gaze.

He was looking up over his shoulder at a range of high woods which fell sharply to a river. At one point a bend of the river bit into the line of the woods, and above the bend rose a cliff, some hundred and fifty feet high. And on the edge of the cliff stood a castle wall.

Neither of us said anything; but, after a little, Mansel started the engine and I put away the map.

Three miles farther on we came to the village of Lerai, where was a bridge. We stopped at the inn there and ordered breakfast, and, while this was being prepared, Mansel talked with the host.

All that we wanted to know, the latter told him. Wagensburg was to be sold: the village postmaster held the keys of the house: no one had viewed the property since it had been for sale. And, when Mansel said he should like to see the castle, the innkeeper called for his hat and set out to find the postmaster and ask for the keys.

When Mansel told me all this – for I cannot speak German, and had understood next to nothing of what had been said – I could have thrown up my hat; and even he was very plainly elated to think that, except for Ellis, our way was so easy and clear. The breakfast was served, but I could hardly swallow for sheer excitement, so that Mansel advised me to think upon fishing and trout streams, "because," said he, gravely, "such contemplation is not only very restful, but very much in point, for, remember, it is trout that has brought us to these parts, and, if we like Wagensburg, we do so because it will make an agreeable fishing-lodge."

Since Mansel never spoke without reason, I strove to do as he said, but I fear my reflections upon angling were incoherent and of no value, for fish are not found in wells, nor do ropes and lanterns form part of an angler's kit. Before, however, the landlord was back with the keys, Mansel had me in hand, and when the former reappeared, I was listening to such a discourse upon flies as must, I think, have interested the most unlikely fisherman that ever was born. To round the picture, the host was brought into the session and made free of Mansel's words, to which, since he was something of an angler, he responded so warmly that I began to think that we should never start, or that, at any rate, Ellis or one of his confederates would first appear.

However, at last we left, with the landlord sitting with Carson in the back of the car.

We crossed the bridge, and, almost immediately leaving the main road, turned to the right up a narrower, rougher way, which, it presently appeared, led only to Wagensburg. For a while the road ran by the river; then it climbed up gradually into the woods and finally lay like a shelf cut out of the side of the forest above the water and tilted up like a ramp to the castle itself. To this there was no gateway, but the road ran right on to the terrace, the wall of which we had seen from the other side. The house was long and low, and stood upon two sides of a pleasant courtyard, to which, upon its third side, the terrace made an apron, with a row of sweet-smelling limes standing between the two. Upon the fourth side stood the stables and the chapel, with a mighty gateway between: through this gateway the road we had used went on, leading so far as I could see, to woods and hanging pastures, and made, undoubtedly, to serve the estate. There were trees in the courtyard, and, a little to one side, by the house, an old parapeted well.

The sun was shining full on the terrace, and Mansel drove into the courtyard and stopped in the shade.

Then we alighted, and the landlord took us over the house.

This was agreeable, and full of fine, big rooms; but there was no running water, and a lot would have had to be done to turn the mansion into a comfortable home.

Mansel, however, seemed well pleased with all that he saw and took good stock of everything, counting up the bedrooms, stepping the salons, and snuffing the air for damp, as though he seriously contemplated taking up residence there for good and all.

At last he turned to the landlord.

"And now about water," he said. "That's so often the stumbling block with these castles up in the hills."

At once the landlord insisted that the supply was superb. No castle in all Carinthia, he declared, was better furnished with water.

"Good," said Mansel, "I'm glad to hear it, because, as a rule, with a well so close to a cliff – "

Here the host interrupted to say that the well in the courtyard had little worth. That, he explained, was the original well; but, as Mansel had surmised, it was dug too close to the cliff, and its gift was meagre and uncertain. *Years ago another well had been dug in the meadows beyond the gateway, a well of great size and depth, the springs of which had never been known to fail, which was so much of a wonder that it was more famous than the castle itself, and was still known thereabouts as The Great Well of Wagensburg.*

"Well, that's all right," said Mansel. "I suppose the water's good."

"The water is excellent, sir, and clear as crystal."

"When was it last cleaned out?"

The landlord threw up his hands.

"Clean out The Great Well of Wagensburg! Why, sir, it is bottomless. I do not suppose it could be done. But the water is perfect: that I will guarantee."

Mansel frowned and put his head on one side.

"All wells should be cleaned from time to time. Never mind. Where does it lie?"

We followed the landlord out of the courtyard, past the chapel and stables and into a wood. Two minutes later we turned into a fair meadow that sloped gently to another wood upon the opposite side. And in the midst of the meadow lay the great well.

When we came near, it was clear that it merited its name.

Twelve feet across it was, with a broad stone parapet about it and a turret-shaped roof above.

Four pillars were supporting the roof, and two of these held the windlass, which was a massive business, laden with a quantity of chain. Bucket there was none, but an empty hook was dangling over the depths.

When he saw there was no bucket, the landlord's face fell; but, after a moment, he said that no doubt it had been put in the stables against being carried off, and, begging us to await his return, started back the way we had come.

While he was gone, we walked to the farther wood and gradually round the meadow, which we found was something of a plateau, for the ground fell away on three sides and only rose on one, that is to say on the side of the farther wood; here it soon rose very sharply into a peak, which commanded a view of the castle and some of the path we had come, as well as for some distance the two approaches to the meadow on which there was no wood.

Whilst we were looking about us, we perceived the landlord returning, bucket in hand, and, when we got back to the well, he and Carson were lowering it into the depths.

The water came up clear and clean and cold, to the great glee of the landlord, who seemed by that circumstance to consider his protests proved, although there was nothing to show how much there was in the well, or whether the water itself was fit to drink. Mansel, however, appeared satisfied, and, after some further discussion, we made our way back to the castle by the path through the wood.

Thence we drove back to Lerai; and presently, having rewarded the innkeeper and declared that, if we bought Wagensburg, he should be our agent for obtaining supplies, left, as was only to be expected, amid a perfect flurry of "nods and becks and wreathed smiles."

As we drove out of the village: "The art of life," said Mansel, "is to make valuable friends."

For the next three hours we proved the country round about, identifying castles and villages and, thanks to the power of the car, covering a great deal of ground. Then at last we turned North and ran into Salzburg that night at eleven o'clock.

Hanbury was glad to see us, and was naturally agog to hear our tale, but he had no news beyond that he had found the offices of the principal house-agents and thought he had seen Ellis at the door of our hotel.

Herein he was right.

When Mansel visited a house-agent on the following day and, after inquiries, announced that he was disposed to purchase Wagensburg, the agent opened his eyes.

"Sir," he said, "you are a few hours too late. Wagensburg is not sold, but it is not for sale. By a curious coincidence I granted an option to purchase this very property yesterday afternoon."

3

The Battle with the Springs

When, ten minutes later, Mansel sat down on a bench and told us that we were forestalled, Hanbury and I stared at each other in dismay.

Before we could speak, Mansel proceeded to take the whole of the blame.

"I chose the wrong evil," he said. "We had six hours' start of Ellis, and I threw it away. I thought I was fighting a battle when I was running a race. And that was a bad mistake. And now we've all three got to think. Ellis has got the wheel, with the Law behind him; we've got the chart. The very least he expects is a compromise."

"Never," I said.

"I agree," said Mansel, "for every reason. And that's why we've got to think how to get the wheel."

He rose then, and, promising to return in half an hour, sauntered away with Tester at his heels.

Hanbury and I sat still in the bright sunshine, saying little, but racking our brains for some way out of the pass.

To me it seemed to be surely a case of stalemate, a position which could only be relieved by our withdrawal from the field. If we had plainly retired, Ellis would hesitate to purchase, for to expend two or three thousand pounds on preventing another from taking what you would like to enjoy is the investment of a Croesus, and, though there was a chance that this purchase would suggest to us the wisdom of coming to terms, to stake so much money so blindly would be unwarrantable. And I think that Hanbury thought the same, for beyond insisting that Mansel had made no mistake, to which I heartily agreed, he only remarked that the race was seldom to the swift, and that he was glad to have seen Salzburg.

The half-hour had not expired before Mansel came back, and, after glancing at his watch, sat down on the bench between us and asked me once again to describe Ellis.

I did so carefully.

"That was the fellow I saw," said Hanbury.

"Very well," said Mansel. "Now, listen. A week ago in London we dined at the Carlton Grill. There and then we agreed to buy Wagensburg, if the place was for sale. At the table next to us was seated a coarse-looking man, who seemed more than once to be listening to what we said. All of us noticed this, but, after we left the grill-room, we thought no more of the matter and went our ways. Yesterday we saw him again in the streets of Salzburg, and it occurs to us that he is the man who holds an option to purchase Wagensburg. If we are right, it is clear that he is no genuine purchaser, but an unprincipled villain, who is merely seeking to enrich himself *at the vendor's expense*." With that he rose to his feet and knocked out his pipe. "And now, we'll go back to the house-agent. We're all very angry, you know, but if I seem too much annoyed you can try to calm me down."

What followed I shall never forget.

By the time we arrived at the office, Mansel was seemingly beside himself with rage, and, when we were presently admitted to the agent's room, he began to storm and rave like any madman. At first, such was his incoherence, that the agent was frightened to death, but, so soon as he gathered that Mansel was not angry with him, but with some common enemy, he became greatly excited, and, apparently catching the frenzy which possessed Mansel, demanded with howls of fury to be informed of the truth. This he was so long denied that I thought he would have lost his reason, for Mansel, while withholding the facts, never ceased to recite the most horrid and galling conclusions, and the unfortunate agent was actually squinting with emotion when Mansel had mercy upon him and told him his tale.

To judge from its effect, he told it very well, for, long before he had finished, the agent's eyes were burning with wrath and indignation, and, when Mansel said he would wager that Ellis had never set foot in Carinthia, much less laid eyes upon Wagensburg, the other screeched that it was true, and that, when he had opened and shown him his book of photographs of properties for sale, Ellis had actually studied the opposite page. That Mansel would not have committed such an error was very obvious, for he had spoken throughout as though he knew Carinthia as well as the palm of his hand, and had constantly referred to castles and villages by name and to Wagensburg itself with a skilful familiarity which would have deceived a Judge. Indeed, all things considered, it was not at all surprising that the agent was swept off his feet and, snatching up a copy of the letter he had yesterday sent to Ellis, thrust it into Mansel's hands and demanded brokenly to be told what he should do.

The letter acknowledged the receipt of five pounds, and stated that, by virtue of having paid that sum, Ellis had secured the sole right to purchase Wagensburg for two thousand five hundred pounds, and that this right would endure for one calendar month.

"Lease me the property today," said Mansel, laying the letter down, "for fifty years at a rent of five pounds a year; in return, I'll undertake, if Ellis doesn't exercise his option – and when he hears of the lease I don't believe he will – to purchase Wagensburg forthwith for three thousand pounds."

For a moment the agent stared, then he began to laugh like a maniac; and Mansel with him.

The two laughed till they cried, as did Hanbury and I, for, though we did not understand what was the joke, unmoved to witness such paroxysms of mirth was beyond our power.

At last: "Prepare the papers," said Mansel, sinking into a chair and taking out banknotes. "I'll give you three hundred pounds as an earnest of the purchase price, to be returned to me if Ellis goes on."

With that, he turned to Hanbury and me and told us what he had arranged, while the agent ran into an adjoining room and began to give instructions to one of his clerks. Very soon we heard a typewriter in action and within half an hour the two Agreements had been signed. Then Mansel wrote the agent a cheque for twenty-five pounds and said that that was compensation for the trouble and annoyance he had caused by discussing his private affairs in a public place; and so we parted, full of goodwill and understanding, which were immensely enhanced by the knowledge that we had undone a common enemy.

At six o'clock the next morning we left for Lerai, servants and baggage and all, in the two cars. We spent the night at the inn, and the next day, in compliance with instructions from Salzburg, the postmaster brought us the keys of Wagensburg.

Be sure we had taken possession within the hour.

To pick our quarters was plainly the first thing to do, and, after a short consideration, we decided to use the kitchen and servants' hall. These were both spacious, and looked not into the courtyard, but on to the woods and meadows towards the great well. They were served by a decent hall, with a house door at either end, and a passage led into the stables by way of a harness-room. All this was very convenient. As well as poss- essing a certain privacy, the rooms were easy of access and could be approached directly from either side of the mansion; once within the stables, the cars would be under our hand; and, whether they were in the kitchen or in the harness-room, where it was arranged they should sleep, the servants would never be more than a few steps away.

So soon as the decision was taken, that part of the house was opened, the stable doors were set wide and the servants fell to cleaning our quarters as hard as they could "for," said Mansel, "once we're dug in, we've little or nothing to fear; but come on a man whose house is out of order, and you've an ally in his camp who is worth as much as yourself."

Then he gave me a map and binocular, and asked me to stay on the terrace as sentinel, desiring me to locate what roads I could see and, when I had done that, to take Tester and prove the ground towards Lerai and see if there was a spot conveniently near from which the village and the bridge could be observed.

Then he and Hanbury began to unload the cars, unpacking the stores which we had bought at Salzburg and disclosing a quantity of stuff which we had brought from England, prominent among which were some electrical apparatus and a great deal of wire.

I saw no more, for I had my work to do, but, when I came back with my report – which was negative, for I could discover no point at all reasonably near from which the village could be viewed – two of the servants were washing the empty cars, the kitchen fire was burning, the hall was full of gear, orderly arranged, a table was set for luncheon under a tree, and the band of a well-known London restaurant was making us free of a selection from *La Bohème*.

When our meal was over, we sat and smoked on the terrace, while the servants were eating theirs, and then, for the first time, I began to appreciate the full charm of our surroundings.

The grandeur of the landscape which the terrace was commanding, as no royal box ever commanded a stage, the dignity of the pleasance upon which we sat, and the high woods all about us, made our present life seem like a handsome dream; and the silence, the sunlight and the sweet air showed me a side of Nature such as I never expected to see anywhere else.

My musing, however, was soon ended, for Mansel asked me to point out the roads I had managed to identify, and, though these were few, before he and Hanbury had imbibed what information I had, the servants had finished eating and Carson and Bell had returned to their work on the cars.

We then went to work with the wire which Mansel had brought, and, after two hours, had laid an invisible trap across the road of approach, and clean around the castle as far as the garden door which we were to use. This we connected to a battery, and then to a bell which hung in the kitchen hall, and, after a little adjustment, to our great content the arrangement worked very well, for the slightest pressure at any point was instantly reported. Then we laid a wire between the stables and the kitchen, and another from the kitchen to the great well, and so established a means of communication which might at any moment prove of great value. When this had been done, we turned our attention to installing electric light, and before sundown our quarters were adequately illuminated, and the searchlight which belonged to the Rolls was able, at our will, to reveal the depths of the well, as I will warrant they had never been revealed before. Then supper was served, and Mansel drew up some orders for the following day. These will sufficiently appear, but he wrote out some general orders which stayed pinned up in the hall, and, so far as I can remember, this was how they ran.

(1) *Reveille at 4 a.m. Breakfast at 7 a.m. Supper one hour after sundown.*

(2) *No light of any kind which can be seen from the courtyard will be shown even for an instant.*

(3) *Accumulators will be charged, if necessary, from 4.15 a.m. and, in any event, each engine will be started and run for five minutes from that hour.*

(4) *So long as any sign of occupation can be seen from the courtyard, the road of approach will be watched.*

(5) *The alarm tape, wires and bells will be tested at reveille, dinnertime and sundown.*

(6) *In addition to their other duties: Carson will take sole charge of the cars and the electrical apparatus, Rowley will act as quartermaster and cook, Bell will clean the quarters and maintain the water supply.*

(7) *No one will leave the castle without acquainting me.*

(8) *The first sign of any approach will be immediately signalled.*

(9) *There will always be someone in the kitchen if there is no one on guard.*

I can remember no more, but these rules show that Mansel did all that he could to guard against surprise and to ensure that our work should go forward with the least embarrassment.

For all that, we were none too well placed. To gain the curtilage of the castle, without being observed, was singularly easy, and the well was two hundred yards from the garden door, so that anyone at all curious and prudent could watch our labour by the hour, and any sudden, determined aggression by three or four armed men would be difficult to counter.

We sat on the terrace for a while before going to bed, and heard some music from London, and at length the news, and but for Mansel, Hanbury and I, I think, would have sat there most of the night, for a full moon was shining out of an empty sky and the prospect which the terrace commanded seemed more lovely than ever.

We were up and abroad the next morning before it was light, and, as soon as the alarms had been tested, repaired to the well.

Mansel had all ready a measuring-line. This was a very fine cord knotted at every inch and tagged at each foot, and at each end was fastened a lump of lead. The use of this proved that what the well-digger had said of its capacity was substantially correct, for the well was two-thirds full of water, and its depth was ninety-six feet. Allowing for the facts that the man would have spoken of metres, and not of feet, and that in so many years a deposit had surely been formed at the bottom of the well, we had no reason to suppose that his actual figures were not as good as ours. Sixty-two feet of water lay in the well.

I have already said that the well was twelve feet across, and, after a moment's calculation, Hanbury drew in his breath.

"That chamber is sealed," he said, "faster, I fancy, than even the well-digger dreamed. If we had a pump – "

"We should be no better off," said Mansel. "A pump can push water, but to pull it up from a depth is beyond its power. If we installed a plant to supply the house, to make sure of water we should have to sink the pump; and no pump that ever was made could empty this well. Whether we can do it by bucket I can't possibly tell, but I'm told that the last six months have been unusually dry, and so, if we go all out, I think we may be able to beat the springs."

Hanbury examined the cupola which sheltered the well.

"We have two pulleys," he said. "If we put a beam across and above the windlass, we can use two buckets together and, with the windlass, three."

"That's right," said Mansel. "And now here's another point. We must make a gutter to take the water away. If we don't do that, it'll find its way back into the well."

Then he picked up a stirrup and, looping the leather onto the hook which was dangling over the well, asked me if I would go down and see what I could.

I was only too ready to comply, but before I descended he made me put on a warm coat against the chill and fastened about me a length of fine rope. I then set my foot in the stirrup and gripped the chain, and Hanbury working the windlass and Mansel paying out the rope, I passed down into the well.

When I was close to the water, I bade them stop, and when they had made all fast, they let down the searchlight.

The well was beautifully built, and I do not believe such masonry is often rendered today. The stones had been finely cut, and, though no doubt they were cemented together, they were fitted so close that the cement did not appear. There were no bars at all, nor any foot or handhold that I could see, but presently I discovered a series of niches regularly cut in the wall, one above the other and about two feet apart. They were scarce an inch deep, and I could not believe that there was any man, living or dead, daring or skilful enough to rise or descend by this means. Happening, however, to look round, I perceived another series, exactly corresponding, a quarter of the way round the well. These were more deeply cut; and it immediately occurred to me that these niches had supported one beam of a wooden stage on which the men had stood whilst building the wall. Sure enough, on the opposite side were the niches for the other beam, one twice as deep as the other; so that, given four clean-cut beams, the men who were working could have raised their stages as they pleased, without any help, two feet at a time. One or two pieces of wood were rotting on the surface of the water, and, here and there, little ferns were growing apparently out of the wall, but otherwise, except that the sides were weather-stained, the well, so far as I could see, was as sound as a bell, and might have only been finished the week before. I could not see the spring working, although I peered very hard, and, since the surface of the water seemed to be motionless, I came to the conclusion that such water as we had drawn had been replaced in the night, and that, having filled this pool to the brim, the little underground stream had resumed its course. And here I soon saw I was right, for there was no watermark above the surface, and the well was plainly full.

All this information I cried to Mansel and Hanbury, and both were greatly delighted at the fine condition of the well; but, as I hung there, seemingly so far beneath them, the magnitude of our task appalled me, and I felt that the silent guardian of the leather bags was to prove a more formidable enemy than Ellis himself.

Then they pulled me up, and the atmosphere seemed sultry after the chill of the well.

Then we went back to the stables, where was some sawn wood, and before it was time for breakfast we had fixed a beam upon the free pillars immediately under the dome, and had lashed a pulley into place upon either side. Whilst we were doing this, Carson and Bell were bringing up planks, of which we had found quite a store, for with these we meant to make a gutter, in the shape of an endless trough, to conduct the water away. By the time we had settled upon the line this should take, it was seven o'clock, so we left the business there and returned to the house.

At breakfast we came to a decision of some importance. This was, plainly, that we should not attempt to conceal our endeavours to empty the well. It was, therefore, arranged that Mansel should drive to Lerai, as soon as he had bathed, and acquaint the landlord of the inn with our intention. He proposed to display great annoyance at being saddled at the outset with such a labour, and, on being asked the reason for our resolve, to say that last night we had drawn up the remains of a baby, which meant, of course, that the whole of the water was foul. He would then procure ropes and buckets and other implements, and even give out that, if after one or two days we needed assistance, he should desire the landlord to find us some men.

So he and Carson left at half past eight, taking the Rolls, whilst Hanbury and I returned at once to the meadow to set to work upon the troughs. With nails and hammer these were easy to make, and, as soon as Bell appeared, we gave him a pick and shovel, and set him to cutting the groove in which our gutter should lie.

Within the hour the bell by the well told us of Mansel's return, and five minutes later we saw him appear in the meadow and come towards us.

"Did that bell ring?" he said shortly.

"Yes," said Hanbury.

"Then, if you please," said Mansel, "never disregard it again."

And there he left it, for as I have said, he was a man of few words; but there was that in his voice which there was no mistaking, and Hanbury and I felt as guilty and ashamed as though by some folly we had ruined our enterprise.

Then he told us that his tale had been well received, and that the landlord seemed genuinely distressed at our predicament, "for such," said Mansel, "he plainly regards it; and when I said that we must empty the well, he threw up his hands. However, when I said that, unless the well could be cleaned, I should give up the place, he sent for buckets and ropes, and promised to come up this evening to see what help he could give. I then sent a wire to Maple's, telling them not to dispatch my furniture; I fear it may puzzle them, but it supported my case and cleared the air."

Here Carson appeared with a bucket as big as a bath; indeed, two men could not have carried it full, but it was made, I imagine, to receive refuse or to hold a store of water upon which a cook could draw. And I must frankly confess that it did my heart good to see it, for I felt that, if we have a giant's task before us, it was something, at any rate, to have a giant's tools to use.

By the time we had finished the gutter, which led down out of the meadow into a kind of combe, it was nearly eleven o'clock, and we sat down and drank some beer which Carson had brought.

Then Bell was sent to the kitchen, and Rowley came up in his stead; Mansel went up to the point in the farther wood, from which, as I have said, a man could observe some of the neighbouring ground; and Carson and Rowley took one rope, and Hanbury and I the other.

The work was hard to the point of severity, but the sight of so much water coming up out of the well was fuel to our endeavours, and we worked for twenty minutes without a break. Long before this Mansel had come to our assistance, for to land the buckets, when full, needed another man, and, lame as he was, he performed this awkward task as he did most things, that is to say, as though he had practised it all his life.

When we stopped for luncheon, we had taken eight feet of water out of the well.

When luncheon was over, we sat on the terrace for a little, under the shade of the limes.

Hanbury was asleep, Mansel was reading *Lockhart's Life of Scott* – without which work, he said, he never travelled, because it was the best host a man's mind could have – and I was lazily regarding the opposing country, when I noticed a patch of haze a great way off. I had hardly remarked it before it disappeared, and it came to me in a flash that it must have been dust. At once I rose and took the binocular, and, since I knew precisely where to look for the road, I was in time to see a closed car flash into and out of view on its journey South.

When I told Mansel, he nodded and said he was glad.

"It's high time," said he. "If they hadn't appeared today, I should have been uneasy. I like the other side to do the obvious thing."

With that he put up his volume, and, asking me to tell him when the car reached the spot from which we had first seen Wagensburg, rose to his feet and began to pace the courtyard, with his hands behind his back and his head in the air.

Presently the closed car appeared beyond the river, and when I reported this, Mansel called the servants, and I roused Hanbury and told him what was afoot.

Then Mansel spoke to us all.

"We are going to be visited," he said, "by five very angry men. I think there'll be five, and I'm sure they'll be angry. This is a good place to receive them for several reasons. I think perhaps I'd better play host, but I shall want some support. Mr Hanbury will take the gateway, and Mr Chandos the road; Carson will take that window, and Rowley that; and Bell will occupy the loft. Please be ready, but nobody show himself until you hear me say 'Now.' And whatever happens, don't fire. I believe in baring the teeth, but to use them, except to bite back, would be very foolish."

Then the stable doors were opened, the Rolls was brought out, and out of her we were armed – the servants with sporting rifles, and Mansel, Hanbury and I with a pistol apiece.

The servants had been through the War, and took this quietly enough, but I never was so much excited in all my life, and pictures of blood-letting and feats of arms rose up before me like so many common rooms of which I had been made free.

Then the car was returned to the stables, and the servants went to their posts, while Mansel showed Hanbury and me how a pistol should be handled, and that the safety-catch was the stile between life and death. After that, Mansel took Tester and shut him up in the house, and, when he came back, we sat down on the wall of the well, by the side of the house, until we should hear the car.

While we were there, Mansel inquired if there was any one line which we thought he should take in dealing with Ellis and his friends, "because," said he, "beyond recommending them to return to the deuce, I've no plan at all. I don't propose to deny that we're looking for treasure, and I propose to announce that we're cleaning the well. If you can't conceal, advertise; it's the next best thing. But I've little else in mind, except that this courtyard is as much as they're going to see."

Hanbury and I had no suggestion to offer, if for no other reason, because to think at all clearly was beyond our power. This mean state of mind, I am sure, was due to our expectation of what was to come, and since this failing is one which I have never cured, I have the more reverence for Mansel who, I think, could await the Powers of Darkness themselves without turning a hair.

Presently we heard the drone of a car climbing into the woods, and Hanbury and I passed out of the great gateway and sat down behind the chapel where we could not be seen.

As I afterwards found, the car contained five men, all of whom alighted, three only of whom spoke. These three were Ellis, the man whom I had knocked down and the other who had answered Mansel at the level-crossing. The last was addressed by his companions as "Rose" – Mansel told us later that he was undoubtedly Rose Noble, a man of some position among thieves – and my friend was called "Punter," though whether that was a nickname I cannot say.

The car came to rest on the terrace, and we heard them alight but for a moment or two they spoke between themselves, as though they had not seen Mansel, and believed the courtyard empty.

Then: "Can I help you?" said Mansel.

When Ellis replied, his voice was shaking, and his speech thick with wrath.

"Yes," he said, "you can. You can pop along off my land. That'll save me the trouble of putting you out."

"Oh, are you my landlord?" said Mansel. "Because, if you are, you can help me to clean out your well. It seems to have been used as a cemetery, and I didn't come here to get typhoid."

Ellis began to rave, but Rose Nobel put him aside.

"What's this wash about landlords?"

"It's very simple," said Mansel, stifling a yawn. "If he owns this estate, he's my landlord. If he doesn't, he isn't. So in any event the question of putting me out will not arise. But I tell you frankly I'm fed up about this well. Supposing – "

"Cut it out," said Rose Noble. "Ellis here's got you down. This place was for sale, and he's bought it."

"And I hold a fifty years' lease," said Mansel. "If he wasn't told, he should have been. But perhaps they thought if he knew he wouldn't buy. And now about this well. When I took the place I was given to understand – "

"You're a great believer in bluff," said Rose Noble.

"You don't believe me?" said Mansel. "Well, that's as you please. But if I am not here of right, why did they give me the keys?"

There was a moment's silence.

Then: "Lease be damned," roared Ellis. "I've bought the — place."

"That gives you," said Mansel, "no shadow of right to be here. Unless I'm behind with my rent, you can't set a foot on this land – for fifty years."

At this there was a great uproar, and I slipped into the road and up as close as I dared, to see that all was well.

Rose Noble and Punter were holding back Ellis, while Mansel was sitting still upon the rim of the well, with one leg cocked over the other, and a pipe in his mouth.

Presently the storm abated, and Ellis suffered Punter to lead him away to the car, on the step of which he sat down and mopped his face, while Rose Noble continued to play the hand.

"Leases and what-not," he said, "don't cut much ice with me. The Law's well enough in its place, but I guess we can do without it this afternoon."

"If you mean," said Mansel, "that you want to stay here and talk, I won't ask you to withdraw for a quarter of an hour."

"That," said Rose Noble quietly, "is exactly what I meant."

With that, he took out a cigar and leaned his back against a tree.

"Do you seriously think," he said, "that we're going to sit right down and let you lift the treasure under our eyes?"

"Not for one moment," said Mansel cheerfully.

"Then," said Rose Noble, "why don't you face the facts. We're five to one and two boys: this isn't exactly Holborn: and we're not afraid to strike."

"I know Ellis isn't," said Mansel.

At that Ellis started up with a volley of oaths, but Rose Noble cursed him into silence, and returned to the charge.

"You know where that treasure is?"

"I do and I don't," said Mansel. "To be perfectly frank, I was going to start looking today, but this infernal well has upset my plans. You must have water, you know."

"Quit that line," said the other sharply. "And tell me – what do you know?"

"Yes, I see the fire-arm," said Mansel. "But it doesn't faze me. Unless I misjudged you, you're not going to make the mistake which was made not far from Chartres three weeks ago."

"How long are we going to stand this?" he cried. "Put it across the — once for all. Shove the cards on the table. I'm sick of being chewed."

Rose Noble disregarded him.

"You drew on me," he said quietly, "by the side of the railway line. You made a hole in my car."

"Two," said Mansel. "Two holes, counting the petrol tank."

The other lighted his cigar.

"Two holes," he said slowly. "And Punter was knocked down. And in spite of all that, I'm going to give you your choice." He threw away the match and folded his arms. "Give us your map or plan or note or whatever it is; give up possession quietly; give me your word to keep out of Austria for the next six months, and I'll let the three of you go."

"I see," said Mansel. "What's the alternative?"

"We take possession," said Rose Noble, "here and now; you will stay *as our guests* until the treasure is found. How long that period will be will depend upon *your ability to withstand the inclination to drink*. When it has been found, and we are gone, your future will depend upon how long it is before somebody passes this way."

I never heard words uttered in a tone so cold and merciless, and Ellis appeared almost genial beside this sinister man.

He was a big, hook-nosed fellow with sandy hair. His face was grey and flabby, and he was very fat. He had a curious way of hooding his eyes, but when he drew back his lids – and this was seldom – you seemed to be looking upon two coals of fire, that were consumed with hatred of everything they saw.

When he had spoken, there was a little silence.

Then: "That's the stuff," said Punter, with half a laugh.

"You think so?" said Mansel swiftly. "Well, we shall see."

He rose. "And now I'm going to be less generous than you. I'm going to give you no choice – except to withdraw. I'm not going to look for the treasure while you sit and watch me do it. I'm in no hurry; in fact, I've time to burn. I've taken a lease on this place for fifty years; the fishing round about here is such as I love, and at the present moment, though it doesn't seem to interest you, I've got my hands full with this well. But don't think, from what I say, that you're free of these grounds. I've a right to order you off, and I'm going to do it *right NOW*. If after this, you return, you'll return as trespassers, and you can take it from me that, so far as this estate is concerned, *trespassers will be shot*."

With that, he looked round the courtyard, and, seeing, I suppose, something in his movement which they did not understand, the five men followed his gaze.

Asprawl in the mouth of the loft, Bell was covering Rose Noble; each of the two open windows was framing a rifle barrel, with a head and shoulders behind; and Hanbury stood in the gateway, and I was in the mouth of the road.

There was a long silence.

At length: "That's two tricks to you," said Rose Noble, rubbing his nose. "But I don't think you'll get any more. An ace

and a King look pretty, but they only take one trick each, and
I'd rather hold the rest of the suit."

"Are you quite sure you do?" said Mansel.

"Yes," said Rose Noble, "and let me tell you this. Before the
game's over you'll remember this afternoon...and the sunshine
...and the air...and the pretty blue sky... And when you
remember them, you'll curse the – that bore you, and — "

Mansel had knocked him down, and, pistol in hand, was flat
against the trunk of the lime-tree against which Rose Noble had
lately been leaning, before a man could cry out or a shot could
be fired. I have never seen any movements so swiftly made;
indeed, looking back at the episode, I cannot honestly say that
I remember it in detail, for, though I was looking on, the matter
was over before I knew it had begun, and I think that the wits
of all present were similarly outrun, for an age seemed to elapse
before Ellis started forward with a yell, and a hand to his hip.

"Don't be a fool," said Mansel, looking along his barrel into
Ellis' eyes. And then: "Put up your hands."

I thought the fellow would have fallen down in a fit, for all the
blood in his body seemed to go into his face, which grew more
black than red, and he put a hand to his throat as though he
were choking.

Rose Noble lay as he had fallen, flat on his back.

"Put up your hands," said Mansel.

Ellis did so.

"You in the cap," said Mansel, addressing the man who had
driven, "take your seat in the car and turn her round."

When this was done, he bade them take up Rose Noble and
put him into the car. They did so. Then he called the bearers to
stand by Ellis' side.

"You three will follow the car, with your hands above your
heads. Drive on."

The car moved off, but for a moment it looked as though the
three pedestrians would rebel. However, I suppose they thought
better of it, for, after looking at one another, like sulky dogs,

with one accord they turned, and, using what dignity they could, walked out of the courtyard and down the road. Carson and Rowley followed as far as the bend; and that was the finish of a passage which was to spoil for ever my enjoyment of "strong" play-acting, be it never so excellently done; for this was the real thing, and to this day the bare remembrance of the affair will quicken the beating of my heart and set my nerves tingling.

Here let me say that Mansel was a good deal troubled about Rose Noble, fearing that the blow he had dealt him might prove fatal for, as I afterwards learned, he had been a famous boxer, but had long abandoned the sport for fear of killing his man.

However, as I shall show, he need have felt no concern.

Before we returned to the well, the six of us sought for points at which a man could play sentry with some success. This was by no means easy because of the woods, but, after a while, we found a ruined shrine on the top of a hill, which commanded the road for some way beyond the bend, and all that side of the estate. The shrine was about six hundred yards from the house but there was no point near one half so valuable. With a sentinel there, we should be safe upon three sides, for to our North lay the river, and from the shrine you could watch the East and South: but the West was the devil. Search as we would, we could find no point at all whence the eye could observe so much as a third of the ground, and I think it would have taken four sentries to make that side secure. We had, therefore, perforce to be content with the hill-top beyond the great well. We did no more than settle these points that afternoon, nor did we visit them again the next day, but thereafter, from dawn to sunset, they were to be regularly occupied. This, to our great inconvenience: but it could not be helped.

We had scarce got back to the well and found that the water had risen eighteen inches in the last three hours, when the landlord of the inn arrived.

He was full of the strangers, who had stopped to ask their way at the inn and had lately returned in such disorder of mind, and was plainly agog to know their business and what was afoot.

We told him that of them we knew nothing till ten days ago, when they had stopped us in a forest with plain intent to rob. We told how we had bayed them, and how I had crippled their car, and supposed that it was sheer rage and a desire to revenge that injury which had induced the villains to dog us to Wagensburg. But, Mansel added, he imagined we had settled their hash, and, unless they were passing venomous, we should not be troubled again.

"All the same," said he, "they are armed, and I'm taking no chances at all. So, when you come up to see us, come by day, for by night all men look alike, and we don't want to hurt our friends."

The landlord seemed perturbed at our tale, because, while Ellis and the driver had presently left in the car, the other malefactors were proposing to stay at his inn. Rose Noble, who was still unconscious, had been carried upstairs to bed, and, though no German had been spoken, the others had made him know that they must have lodging and food. They had not asked for a doctor, and seemed untroubled by the condition of their friend; except for one battered suitcase, they had no luggage; their manner was overbearing and such as might be expected of lawless men.

We purposely offered him cold comfort, and, such was his agitation to think that he had been saddled with such undesirable guests, that the poor man displayed little interest in what he had come to see, and, merely inquiring what headway we were making against the springs, abstractedly accepted an order for supplies and set off on his way back to Lerai, like a man in an ugly dream.

By sundown we had taken another seventeen feet of water out of the well.

We were so much exhausted with our labour that not one of us was fit to descend, but we were all highly pleased to think that our net gain that day had been twenty-three feet and a half, and that now but thirty-nine feet of water remained in the well. Indeed, though no one said so, I believe each hoped in his heart that by the evening of the next day we should discover the shaft.

I suppose, that in view of our progress, it was natural to nurse such hopes, for, though we knew that the water would rise in the night, we had so far no knowledge of the well beyond that it had a reputation which had never been determinedly attacked; but our chagrin in the morning was the more bitter, and it was when we pulled up our measuring-line in the grey of the dawn that for the first time we knew that, when the Count committed his two leather bags to the well, he made them wards of a Court which respected no man, which just and unjust alike might seek to move in vain.

The forces of Nature were against us, and whilst we slept, the springs had undone our labour, much as Penelope unravelled her famous web.

During the night, the water had risen no less than thirteen feet.

This was a great blow, for, though we were yet ten feet six to the good, it showed that the day before we must have passed springs which gave at a great pace, and that it was more than likely that the lower we went, the slighter would be our gain, until at length we should lose as much by night as we had won by day. In that case, the shaft would only be discovered by a furious spell of work, at the end of which, however exhausted we might be, an effort to reach the chamber would have to be instantly made, while those who did not descend must cease-lessly labour to keep the water down, and so save their fellows from being trapped.

Now, this was all conjecture, to which, I fancy, the dreariness of the hour and a threatening sky made generous godmothers, but there was no blinking the facts that our supper and a short night's rest had proved extremely expensive, and that, without a sufficiency of food and sleep, we should never be able to counter the activity of the springs.

That any of the thieves would return to trouble us this day seemed so improbable that we took no precautions beyond keeping a servant in the house, and, except that Hanbury and Carson spent an hour laying wire to the west of the castle, to complete our system, we were five to fight the water all day long.

When, half an hour after sunset, the last bucketful was pulled up, there were only nineteen feet of water left in the well.

Had it been possible, we would have returned after supper and made one mighty effort to reach the shaft, but, though Mansel and Carson and I could, I believe, have continued, George Hanbury and Rowley and Bell could hardly stand for fatigue, and would, I think, have fallen asleep at their work: and, since to ask men so weary to play sentry would have been waste of breath, there was nothing to do but look forward to the following day.

Mansel, however, consented to my going down the well, to see what was to be seen, and locate, if I could, with a bar the mouth of the shaft.

Carson made a small seat, like that of a swing; and this was made fast to the chain. Beneath the seat was a hook, and on this we hung the lamp, the bar we lashed so that it dangled below, just clear of my feet. Then I put on a coat and a lifeline, and they let me down.

The journey seemed unending, and I soon unhooked the lamp and looked about me whilst I was going down.

The condition of the masonry was as perfect as it had been above, but between most of the edges of the stones a thin blade of a knife would have passed, and this, I suppose, meant that they had been laid without cement to suffer the entry of the springs. That these were active was manifest, for fifty feet down the walls were running with water; but there was no gush anywhere, and where the great springs rose I could not tell. When I came to the pool, it was troubled on every side, yet so faintly that, had I not already known what to expect, I would not have believed that so unobtrusive an industry could have been so swift and masterful.

I then hung up the searchlight, and took hold of the bar, and, signalling them to lower me till the water was over my knees, began to seek the shaft with all my might. But everything was against me. The bar was too short and too heavy; the water seemed like treacle to my weary arms; if I leaned to one side, my seat swung at once to the other, as though it would cast me out. At last, by rocking myself to and fro, I managed to sound every side for about three feet; but I could do no better and, when I had almost lost my seat for the second time, I took a last look round and gave the signal for the others to pull me up.

Now, I had looked to see if the niches I had found in the sides the day before ran all the way down the well; and I had found that they did so. But not until I was rising did it occur to me that, as the niches had been used, so they could serve again, and that the value of a stage, however rough, from which to search for the shaft or conduct any operations would be inestimable. Before, therefore, they landed me, I begged Mansel to send for a lath with which I might measure how long the beams must be; and, after a little, he let me have my way.

The measurement took some time, for, remembering how nearly I had twice lost my seat, I dared make no movement at all except with my hands, and Mansel and Carson had to hold me close to the wall. Then I could not see, until they had fixed the light, and twice the lath had to be returned and sawn to another length. However, at last it was over, and I was pulled up. And, after supper, that night Carson and I cut two rafters out of an outhouse roof; and, since of the wood in the stables three planks remained, before we lay down to sleep we had our stage.

4

The Attack on the Well

During the night the water rose twenty feet.

It went against the grain to post two sentries, when with twelve, or even ten, arms we might have had the wall empty by four o'clock. But to be surprised at such gruelling labour would have meant for us the end of everything; for, shaken and stripped and breathless, we could have put up no fight, and, except for the parapet of the well, there was no cover to hand.

Still, it seemed very likely that four of us, working hard, would be able to draw so much water before the sun went down that, with the help of the stage, we should find the mouth of the shaft. And, once we knew on which side of the well that lay, though the springs should deny us passage, at least we should have a second string to our bow.

With this object, we laboured till lunch-time, like men possessed – at least, Mansel and the servants laboured, whilst I sat above on the peak with a rifle across my knees. Hanbury was at the shrine.

At one Rowley took my place, and Carson Hanbury's.

This relief had not long been done, and we were at lunch in the meadow, when – as Hanbury had told us would happen, for he had seen him *en route* – the landlord of the inn arrived.

As he emerged from the wood, he looked around him, and, when he saw us at meat, he threw up his hands.

I felt sure, as did Mansel, that Rose Noble was dead, but it soon appeared that the fellow was only distressed to find that our zeal to attempt to empty the well was unabated.

"Sirs," he cried, bubbling, "it is dreadful to see you so bent upon so hopeless a task. You are killing yourselves in vain. I have sought everywhere for helpers, but, when I tell them for what their help is required, they laugh me to scorn. You will not get a man in all Carinthia. And the trout lie in the streams about you, thick as autumn leaves."

Mansel laughed.

"The springs are the devil," he said, "but we haven't given up hope."

"Ah, sir," said the innkeeper, "but listen. You have not begun. You are still dealing with the first spring. When you are twenty feet down – "

"Make it forty," said Mansel. "To be exact, forty-three."

Lest he should think we were boasting, we took him to the well and showed him the measuring-line. His amazement was ludicrous, for he seemed unable to speak and gaped upon us as though we were demigods; and such in his sight, I suppose, we were, for in three days we had gone far to shatter a tradition which had endured for a century and a half.

Then Mansel asked him of his guests. Of these he spoke abstractedly; but we learned that Rose Noble was recovered, and that Ellis had come back this morning and taken the three away – he knew not whither, but imagined to Salzburg. They had paid him nothing for their lodging, of which they had constantly complained, but had made him understand that they would come back. What more he said I cannot remember, save that the stores we had ordered were piled by the kitchen door, and after a little he left, still plainly bewildered by the progress which we had made.

I was for instantly withdrawing the two sentinels and making a mighty effort to get the treasure that night, but to this Mansel would not consent, for fear that Rose Noble and Ellis were not gone at all, but had pretended departure in the hope that the news would reach us and throw us off our guard. He suggested, instead, that Hanbury and I should only work for two hours, and should then relieve Carson and Rowley, "for in that way," he said, "at sundown Carson and Rowley will be done and can go to bed, but you and Hanbury will be as fresh as paint; and, if Bell and I go gently this afternoon, we shall still have something to spare at nine o'clock."

To Hanbury and me this arrangement seemed more than good, except that we both begged Mansel to give himself a rest. But of this he would not hear. For the next two hours, therefore, we worked as hard as we could, but the honours of that day went to Carson and Rowley, for, while I sat on my hill-top, I could hear them at work, and, knowing how severe was the labour, I would not have believed that two men could maintain the pace they did for nearly five hours.

When I came in at sundown, the two were ready to drop, but they looked very pleased, and Mansel told me with a smile that they had uncovered the shaft.

Half an hour back, he said, the suck and gurgle of air disputing with water had told its tale, and, though to ascend at once might be impossible, enough of the mouth was open for us to survey the shaft.

Then Hanbury and I made haste to fetch the stage, and Carson and Rowley were ordered back to the house. They were reluctant to go, but Mansel was determined that they should have food and rest, "and, if you stay here," said he, "you will have neither, but will drift into helping us when you're too tired to help yourselves. It's possible that we may need you in two hours' time; so go and eat and sleep, while you have the chance."

Bell and Tester went with them, for Bell was to keep watch and prepare some food, and Tester was to be tied up, because he was sure to be distressed if Mansel went down the well and might even fall down in some effort to comfort his lord.

Then I went down, with the light and the beams which Carson and I had cut the night before.

A foot or more of the mouth of the shaft was visible, and, by directing the light, I could see the steps within; but I never beheld a place which looked so black and uninviting, and there was now in the depths of the well an odour which I cannot exactly describe. It seemed to be a bad smell, grown faint with age.

I had my beams in place in a minute of time, and then gave the signal for Hanbury to lower the planks.

As might have been expected, the shaft was between the two beams, but so much had I twisted and turned during my descent that, though I knew from the niches that it must run North or South, I could tell no more. But, when the planks were in place, Mansel lowered the measuring-line, and under my direction, moved it until it hung plumb over the middle of the mouth. This showed, as I afterwards found, that the shaft ran North, towards the castle: and Hanbury marked the place by driving a peg out of sight into the ground.

The stage, when I had built it, lay some six inches below the lintel of the mouth of the shaft. The water was rising fast, and I set the planks as close to the mouth as I could, so that by using the windlass, without disturbing the stage, we could do something to keep the water down.

Then I was pulled up, and Mansel made ready to descend.

Over his clothes he put on a waterproof suit, tight-fitting at the wrists and ankles as at the waist and throat. In his pocket he had a torch, and that was all.

Communication by shouting up and down the well had proved unsatisfactory, for the words arrived distorted and often unrecognizable: while I was below, therefore, Mansel and

Hanbury had lashed a spring to the pulley-beam and fastened a cord to the spring. This rude apparatus worked very well, for, when the cord was pulled tight and then let go, the spring hit the beam with a smack which there was no mistaking. To the other end of the cord was fastened a biscuit-tin, which, in case of trouble, we were to dash against the wall. We also took the bell which rang from the kitchen hall and hung it inside the parapet so that, were it to ring while he was below, Mansel would receive so important a signal direct.

So soon as Mansel was down, we were to start bailing, and the signal that he was clear and that we could pull up the seat was to be two strokes of the spring upon the pulley-beam.

We had hardly begun to lower him, when, to our dismay, the searchlight, which I had left burning upon the stage, went suddenly out; but Mansel cried to us to go on, and a moment later I saw the flash of his torch. Compared with the searchlight, this threw a miserable beam; and I was not at all happy to think he was going down thus embarrassed to a place which had seemed so dreadful when it was full of light. I think we all had three hopes that, when he was down, he would be able to put in order what had gone wrong, but, if we had, they were vain, for, after a little, the spring struck twice upon the beam, and, when we pulled up the seat by which we had let him down, the lamp was hanging upon the hook beneath.

Then we let down a bucket and started to bail, and we knew that Mansel was in the shaft, for the light which his torch had been giving had disappeared.

And, except that we laboured steadily for about five minutes, that is as much as I know of that day's work, for then I was dealt such a blow on the back of my head that I fell down like an ox and lost consciousness.

Hanbury saw me fall, but before he had time to cry out, he had been served as I had, and, since he was still senseless when I sat up, Mansel alone of us three can speak to what followed the assault.

This was the tale he told us so soon as he could.

"I made a bridge of a plank from the stage to a step in the shaft, and so spared myself immersion; and, though I got pretty wet, I was able to keep the torch out of the water. Then I drew the plank after me into the shaft, for, if I had left it in place, the bucket would have fouled it when you began to bail.

"The shaft is three feet wide by about five high. Its walls and steps are of stones from the river-bed, laid in cement. Its roof is curved and built of stones similar to those used for the well. I imagine it owes its style to the Count's desire for secrecy, for all the stuff used to build it might well have gone into the well. The walls of the latter are certainly backed with pebbles as high as the first spring.

"The going was very unpleasant, not to say dangerous, for the steps are very rough and covered with slime. I had hoped, by counting them and measuring the rises and treads, to get figures from which Hanbury could tell pretty well where the chamber lies, but their flight is so irregular that without a rule I could do nothing valuable. So far as I could make out, the shaft runs dead straight. The air was abominable.

"I had taken some twenty-five steps before I slipped.

"Now a fall in that shaft would be an ugly business, and I don't think you could complain if you broke no more than a leg, and, as, all things considered, it's not the place you'd choose for a first-class smash, I saved myself at the cost of dropping the torch. This, of course, was broken by the fall, and, although I recovered it, it would give me no light.

"To proceed in the dark seemed futile, and I had just begun to retrace my steps, when I became aware of a light which came from the well.

"I at once assumed that you had adjusted the searchlight and were letting it down, for I heard the windlass working, but a moment later I thought that I heard a whistle, and stopped in my tracks.

"Someone alighted heavily on the stage.

"But for the whistle I had heard, that it was not you, Chandos, would never have entered my head. As it was, I made sure you would hail me almost at once, but, remembering that all things are possible, I waited for you to speak.

"That I did so was just as well, for I was still waiting when somebody snuffed and spat.

"Well, that eliminated any of us.

"I can't pretend I wasn't shaken.

"I dared not think what had happened to you and Hanbury; the servants, presumably, were obediently keeping the house; the enemy had the windlass; and I was trapped, good and proper, in a blind tunnel five by three, and eighty-odd feet below ground.

"All of a sudden I wondered if the enemy knew I was there.

"I decided that the odds were that he did not. Unless he had seen me go down, there was no reason why he should know. The searchlight had failed, my torch had gone out, although the stage was there, I had withdrawn my bridge. The fact that he made no attempt to conceal his presence assured me that I was right.

"Instinctively I began to reascend the shaft.

"I had not thought that even Rose Noble would suspect our work at the well, and the reflection that I had been so heartily outwitted and outclassed was very bitter. The attack had been well done. One minute, you and Hanbury were bailing, the next, one of the five was descending the well. I assumed that he had come to reconnoitre. When he had made his report, the others would bail for a while, and then the actual attempt to lift the treasure would be made. Unless I could reach the servants, I did not see how this could fail.

"I had taken five or six steps, when a splash told me that my man was making the shaft. Though there was still one spare plank, the idea of a bridge had not, I suppose, occurred to him, but, after a struggle – in which he went under water – I heard him make the steps. For a moment he stood grunting and blowing, and trying to get his breath. Then he began to ascend. This surprised me, for I had made certain that he would first produce a torch, but what astonished me still more was the progress he made, for he climbed as well as I had when I had seen my way.

"So we went up the shaft in single file, some thirty odd steps apart.

"My own idea, of course, was to get to the top of the well. The only way to do this was, unknown to the rest of the gang, to take his place and let them haul me up in his stead. What would happen when they saw their mistake no one could tell, but with luck I should have been landed before they saw what they had done.

"It was quite plain that, if I could escape the notice of the man in the shaft, I should stand a better chance of taking his place. Even if I had room, I could not see to hit him under the jaw, unless I could knock him senseless, he would probably let out a yell; I was unarmed, and by a hand-to-hand fight in the dark in such a place I was as likely to come to harm as was he. But what weighed with me most of all was the natural reluctance to kill. Unless I laid him out, his shouts would give me away; but, if I put him out of action, in view of the pace at which the water was rising, he would either be drowned or trapped – probably trapped. And it seemed a shocking thing to sentence a fellow creature to such a terrible doom.

"To avoid him in the shaft was out of the question, but I thought if I could reach the chamber, I could let him go by to the treasure and start right back.

"I was not afraid of his hearing me, for I was going quietly, but he made a lot of noise.

"The shaft seemed endless, but at last I felt a step which was clear of ooze. I took it, and two more, and then something I hadn't expected told me that I was upon the threshold of the chamber itself. *Four iron bars, set up on end in the way*. From their shape, I should say they were crowbars, such as a well-digger used about his business. And I don't suppose it took five minutes to bed them, but, once the cement had set, well, I don't know if you've ever filed iron, but it's tedious work. Top and bottom, they were bedded into hewn stone. There's no doubt about it, Axel the Red was a very careful man.

"That it would come to a fight was now certain; so I set my back to the bars and awaited my man.

"Suddenly I heard the bell ring at the top of the well.

"My man heard it, too, and stopped – about ten steps away.

"Of course, I knew what it meant, and praised God. But he was clearly alarmed, for he was holding his breath, and, I fancy, straining his ears. I know exactly how he felt, and, believe me, I don't blame him.

"The bell rang again.

"A moment later I heard him begin to descend.

"Be sure I followed.

"Before I did so, I tested every bar. They were all the same size, nearly an inch thick, not very rusty: and not one of them would budge.

"Such plan as I now had was to follow him into the well. When he had been reassured by those at the top, I thought it more than likely that he would re-enter the shaft and try once again to reach the chamber, but, whether he did or no, once I was in the well, I should be immeasurably better placed to deal with whatever arose, if for no other reason, because to occupy that shaft, yet not dwell upon its undesirability as a retreat is almost impossible.

"And here let me say that, treasure or no, I was immensely surprised to find that any one of the five could withstand its terrors so well. Of the ugly side of Nature that kind of man usually fights very shy. Ellis, for instance, would never have gone down the well. I knew it wasn't Rose Noble, and Punter would have cursed; but, whichever of the others it was, he was a brave man, for, if the devil had not been driving, I wouldn't have gone up that shaft without a light for any money.

"The fellow descended steadily, and I came down after as fast as I dared.

"At last I heard him touch water. Then he took a deep breath and floundered out of the shaft. By the time he was on the stage I was still ten steps up. The water had risen, for they had not thought to bail, and the stage was submerged.

"I made what haste I could, but I heard no colloquy. I imagine that he whistled, but, as I slid into the water, the windlass began to work; and, when I took hold of the stage and could look about me, I saw my man in mid-air, lantern and all.

"I did not know whether to be sorry or glad, but what was much worse, I did not know what to think. What mystified me was their silence. This seemed unnatural, and I could think of no reason why they should take him up without a word.

"I had pulled myself on to the stage and was listening to the click of the ratchet and watching the lantern rise, when, all of a sudden, I heard the windlass stop.

"Then a shot was fired, and, after a moment, I heard a flurry of voices at the top of the well.

"I assumed that the servants had come to dispute possession of the windlass, and, generally, counter the attack; and I would have given a lot to be above ground, but, all the same, it struck me that, ill placed as I was, I would very much sooner be standing upon the stage than dangling from the end of the chain some forty feet up.

"I had just come to this conclusion when the man who was in mid-air expressed the same view; at least, from the apprehension with which he invested an oath, I gathered that he felt his position. And, directly I heard his voice, *I knew who it was*. And the knowledge, as you may imagine, gave me plenty of food for thought.

"So I stood very still and waited, with my eyes on the lantern and my back against the wall."

That was as much as Mansel had to tell, and, since there was but one shot fired at that time, I can take up the story without a break, because I had just sat up and was trying to collect my wits, when I heard a cry and men running, and then the sound of a shot.

The moon had not yet risen, but I could make out the well and that I was sitting above it, half in and half out of the wood. My wrists were bound behind me, and my head was aching very much.

There were figures about the well, and I heard Rose Noble's voice.

"Who fired?" he said. "We or they?"

"I did," said Punter. "They saw me coming and ran."

"Pardon me," said Rose Noble: "they heard you. You don't know how to move. How many were there?"

"Two," said Punter. "Servants, I think; but it may have been the two pups."

"That's right," said another voice. "They was busy crankin' the well."

Here one of them must have looked down and seen the light, for there was a cry of surprise, and then a buzz of exclamation, of which I could make no sense.

Then Rose Noble spoke again.

"Quite so," he said. "Quite so. If there's one down there, we've got him by the short hairs. And is that as far as you can see? Damn it," he cried, "lift up your – eyes! THINK! *What are they doing by night in this well*? You may have a twist for sweet water, but – "

The rest of his sentence was drowned in a burst of appreciation of his discovery; and I never heard grown men so abandon themselves to their glee, for they shouted and stamped and laughed, like so many lunatics, and nothing that Rose Noble could do could bring them to order.

In the midst of the flurry another came running up, and then I heard Ellis' voice.

As far as I could make out, they were now all five by the well, but, since they all continued to speak at once, I could hear nothing that was said.

Then Ellis was asked some question, and I heard his reply.

"I think they're out," he said. "There's no light or sound. When I tried the door, a dog barked: but that was locked, and the ground-floor windows are barred."

"There's three of them somewhere," said Rose Noble. "Two of them ran from here, and there's one below."

"God give it's Little Willie," said Ellis, and sucked in his breath. "I'd like to meet him like this."

"Me, too," said Punter.

"Big Willie, you mean," said Rose Noble. "Bag him, and we've got the lot. Besides," he drawled, "if anyone's thinking of scores, I reckon I've one to settle that takes precedence."

The oath with which he enforced this dark saying was the most dreadful I've ever heard, and I began to strive, like a madman, to free my wrists, for the thought that Mansel was about to deliver himself into such cruel and bloody hands was insupportable.

"Job," said Rose Noble, "back to the path and watch. If anything moves, let it have it: we don't want to be disturbed."

Here one of them found the searchlight, and they wasted a minute or two trying to make it light. Then they kept peering down the well and whispering and cursing one another for making a noise. Indeed, I never saw men so plainly out of their element, for they did not seem to remember that those they had put to flight had been using the windlass, or to notice what must have been manifest – that the lantern below them was nowhere near the water: and it was only after a lot of argument that two took hold of the windlass and felt the weight on the chain.

"It's loaded," I heard one say. " 'Eavy as lead."

At that they all peered over the parapet again, and I did not know what to think, but was greatly afraid that the weight must be Mansel himself.

Here my attention was diverted to something which stirred by my side. To my relief, it proved to be Hanbury, bound as was I. I managed to move until I had my mouth to his ear, and, as soon as he could receive it, I told him as much as I knew. Except that his head was aching, he did not seem to be hurt, and, when I suggested that I should try to unfasten the cord which was binding his wrists, he turned on his side and put them up without a word. At once I turned my back on him and got to work upon the knots, but I made no progress, and, after a minute or so, his fingers brushed mine aside, and fell to work in their stead.

At that moment I heard Rose Noble say "Give way," and at once two men at the windlass began to turn.

The moon was rising now, and I could see that the others were on their knees or crouching beside the parapet, ready, no doubt, to cover Mansel the moment he reached the top. That they thought this was necessary argues their respect for his arm, for even they must have realized that four men can never have had one at a great disadvantage.

Hanbury worked feverishly, while I tried to think what to do.

Unless he were in danger of death, to attempt to assist Mansel until we had arms of some sort, would be the act of a fool. I, therefore, decided that, when once we were free, we must try to reach the kitchen, join forces with the servants, and deliver a counter-attack.

Hanbury had freed me, and I was wrestling with his bonds, when a faint light began to appear within the well.

This horrified us both, for we thought, of course, that it was that of Mansel's torch; and that he should show a light which could assist none but his foes was not his way. Indeed, we now fully expected any moment to hear him address us, and ask why on earth we had kept him waiting so long.

The glow in the well was very definite when at last I had Hanbury free, and at once we crept out of the wood and began to crawl by its edge towards the house.

I was in front, and going as fast as I dared, when I came face to face with Bell, who was crawling the opposite way. The first I knew of it was the barrel of a pistol pressed tight against my temple, for he had seen me coming, and had not known who it was.

Then, lying there, I told him as much as I knew, and he said that Carson and Rowley had taken up positions on either side of the path. He was to crawl to where he could see and hear what was going on at the well, and, at a flash from his torch the three were to count two seconds and then open fire. The idea was to drive the thieves into the combe into which the gutter ran, but at any cost to keep them away from the house and out of the two woods, for that would give a chance of rescue to the occupant of the well.

I at once fell in with his plan, whereupon we decided that I should take his place. He, therefore, gave me his torch and one of the pistols he had, and, when I had arranged for him to give his other to Hanbury, and then return to Carson, I went about. As I passed Hanbury, I told him that Bell was there and, when he had got his pistol, to stay where he was.

I had hardly done so when a sudden clamour arose at the top of the well. The light was gone, but all four men were peering at something within.

At length: "Haul him in," said Rose Noble.

They were very inexpert and mortally afraid of falling, and hard words were exchanged and much swearing before their burden was landed roughly enough, with two on the top of him and the other two standing by.

Before a torch could be lighted, Punter let out a yell. "By —," he cried, "it's that — that keeps the inn!"

To me his words came like a thunderbolt, and, between my relief and my astonishment, for a moment I felt quite dazed.

Then it occurred to me that this was the moment to attack and that a sudden assault, coming upon them while they were so much engaged with the turn events had taken and were still uncertain what to think or do, would probably fare better than we could have hoped; so I took my pistol and torch, and, directing the face of the latter towards the house, gave the agreed signal, counted two seconds, and fired.

This was as Carson had arranged, and nothing could have been better, for the five of us fired almost at once, and so unexpected a volley would, I should think, have disconcerted a Napoleon himself.

No one fell, and, without so much as a cry, the four thieves scattered and ran straight for the combe – *with the innkeeper pelting behind*. Two of them fouled the gutter and fell to glory, but, perhaps because they had run into the moonlight, they were not content to lie, and, picking themselves up, rushed violently after their fellows down the slope, like the Gadarene swine. This much I saw, for I had run along by the edge of the wood, and I sent a shot after them, before hastening to the well.

The seat was not on the hook, but only a bight of rope, so that, had I not seen him run, I should have thought that the innkeeper was ready to drop with fatigue; but we had the seat slung in a twinkling, and Carson and Rowley lowered it into the well.

I must confess that I waited in fear and trembling, for I knew that the water must have risen a foot or more, and the thought that the landlord had emerged alive from the well filled me with the gravest misgivings for Mansel's safety. I was also quite sure that the thieves would presently return, when, if we had not raised Mansel, we should present to them as fair a target as they had offered us, and the likelihood that they would bungle a second and better chance seemed small indeed.

When the seat was nearly down, Hanbury took hold of the signal cord and swung the biscuit-tin, and a moment later, to our indescribable relief, the spring struck once upon the beam.

At once we locked the windlass; and, in an instant, another two blows gave us the signal to hoist.

Then we all five fell upon the windlass, and brought Mansel up with a run, and, only waiting to take up the searchlight, the seat, the measuring-line and the bell, we left the meadow in good order, with Carson, rifle in hand, bringing up the rear.

Two minutes later we were within the house, where Tester greeted Mansel as though in fact he knew that he was risen from the dead.

Here I will say what I should have set down before, namely, that the walls of the kitchen-quarters were immensely thick, and must have formed part of the castle which was burned down. The windows were high above ground and heavily barred, and, since we had hung up curtains some distance away from the frames, neither by day nor night could anyone from without see into the rooms.

Then supper was served, and Mansel and Bell and I told each his tale.

Bell had little to add to what I now knew; but one thing that he said we all found interesting, and that was that the second attack had undoubtedly come from the South, that is to say, from the combe into which we had packed the thieves, "for," said Bell, "although the alarum bell went, it went but once, and I think it was rung by one man coming up from the West, but, when the innkeeper's party took to their heels, then ran North by the path through the woods and past the house: and, since I am sure that was not how they had come, they must have done so because they were driven that way."

Only when all had been said, did I remember Job.

When I spoke of him, Carson smiled.

"I heard what Rose Noble said, sir, so it was hardly fair. He said 'Back to the path, and watch,' *so I did as he said.*"

"I hope you didn't kill him," said Mansel.

"Oh, no, sir," said Carson. Then he hesitated. "I was going to ask you, sir – supposing it had been Rose Noble…?"

Mansel shook his head.

"Certainly not," he said. "And here let me say you can all of you thank your stars that you're such bad shots. I don't wish to sound ungrateful, but, unless I'm being tortured, you must leave these volleys alone. That's the way people get hurt. *Except in the last resort, you are never to fire to hit.* That is the handicap or disadvantage of – "

As Tester growled, some object parted the curtains, and fell clean on to a loose cushion which belonged to the Rolls.

The terrier leapt at it, but, before I could think, Mansel had sent him flying and, with a great cry of "DOWN!" had hurled the thing into the kitchen and fallen upon his face.

The next instant a most frightful explosion shook the house, which I verily thought was coming about our ears; for the lights went out and the whole of the plaster of the ceiling in the servants' hall fell down on our heads; and, what with the concussion and the dust and the tinkle of falling glass and the sudden return of the pain in the back of my head, my wits very nearly left me, and, when I heard Mansel speaking, he seemed to be a great way off.

"Is anyone hurt?" he said, and called the roll.

Mercifully, no one was touched, for we had been all six in the servants' hall; and, when he called Tester, I heard the dog rush in answer to lick his face.

"That was a bomb," said Hanbury dazedly.

"That was a bomb," said Mansel. "And now I withdraw what I said a moment ago. *You can shoot Rose Noble and Ellis as soon as you get the chance.*"

I have tried to analyse the feelings of us all at that time, with poor success.

Whether the lust for gold had mastered us, whether a hatred of the thieves suffused our outlook, whether their attempts to thwart it had but toughened our resolve I cannot say: but I know that after the bomb had been thrown into our midst, we would, one and all, have died in agony rather than let the treasure fall into the enemy's hands.

That we found the act an outrage was, I think, reasonable; we had certainly fired upon them, as Mansel had warned them we should do; but that we had done in the open, where they had a good chance of escape and every opportunity of defending themselves. In return, they had taken a weapon of a barbarous kind, and had used it in circumstances so favourable to its energy that, had it not fallen where it did, and had the room door been shut, we must all six have perished miserably.

In view of what had happened since sundown, we knew that one phase of our struggle had come to an untimely end. Our cake, so nearly baked, had fallen back into dough, and every plan we had made was now impracticable. But, in spite of all there was to be decided, we were too much obsessed and confounded by the attempt which had so nearly made an end of us all to bring our minds to bear at all profitably upon other matters. Add to this that Mansel was physically worn out, and that Hanbury and I were suffering from the blows we had severally received.

We, therefore, lay down to sleep in the harness-room, to which, directly after the explosion, we had withdrawn. Tester was put in the Rolls, to watch the stables, and the servants were to take turns of guarding the passage which led to the kitchen hall. Yet, weary as we were, for a long time we could not sleep; and, ridiculously enough, Hanbury and I were greatly troubled by thirst; but, since our store of water stood in the kitchen, there was nothing to be done, for, supposing it was still available, no one could have reached it in silence or without showing a light.

5

We Go to Ground

By the time I awoke the next morning some order had been restored, and a table, upon which Rowley was serving breakfast, had been set in the harness-room. My head was sore and tender, but did not ache, and, though I would have liked to go out and breathe some fresh air – for neither by door nor window did the harness-room give upon the outside of the castle – I felt very little the worse for anything that had happened the night before.

Then Mansel and Hanbury appeared from the kitchen hall, and I learned that Carson and Bell were guarding the kitchen-quarters from the first floor of the house. To command the courtyard was simple, for this could be done from any window that looked upon it; and, as luck would have it, the South-West corner of the castle ran into a staircase-turret, from which anyone approaching the kitchen from the meadow side could be easily shot down.

There was, of course, a very great deal to be settled, but we had but to raise one issue to perceive that its consideration was depending upon our determination of another, and, by the time we had breakfasted, we had done little but agree upon two or three matters of fact.

The innkeeper knew of the treasure and where it lay. How he had learned the secret, it was idle to speculate; as like as not, he had held it for years, but, because he would not share it except with his two confederates, he had perforce been content to let the treasure lie. How nearly we had played into his hands was a disturbing thought.

The thieves as good as knew where the treasure lay; and, in view of what had to be done to reach the chamber, it seemed probable that they would press the innkeeper into their service: knowing what manner of men they were, the fellow would go reluctantly.

Our party, alone of the three, knew of the iron bars. This knowledge was of great value, for it showed that any dash for the treasure was doomed to failure, and that, even if we still had the well, unless we could work undisturbed, our chances of lifting the bags by way of the shaft would be almost negligible. Mansel had watched the water, whilst he was down in the well, and at the mouth of the shaft it rose at the pace of at least thirty inches an hour: and, since to cut through one bar would take the best part of three hours, such a load of labour, coming at the end of an exhausting day, would be more than five men could carry, unless they had each one the strength and endurance of a giant. And that would mean posting but one sentry, which was unthinkable.

Even reinforced by the landlord, the thieves would not labour as we had. For one thing, they had neither the physique nor the condition of body which we enjoyed; for another, they were out of their element. For all that, we hoped very much that they would make an attempt to re-empty the well, for that would keep them occupied and leave us more or less free to go about our business of finding another way. For that, if we were not to abandon the enterprise, we must clearly do.

And here we stepped into a very slough of difficulty; for, without the enemy's knowledge, to drive a new shaft to the chamber was demanding the cunning of an Odysseus, and how, in the face of such aggression as we had met the night before, we were at once to prosecute such travail, hold the stables and maintain our supplies was a question which not one of us could pretend to answer. And yet, as luck would have it, thanks to George Hanbury's most intelligent observation, this Gordian knot was unloosed within the hour.

When we had breakfasted, Mansel desired Hanbury to relieve Carson, and me to take Bell's place, so that the two could come down and get some food, and it was half an hour later, when Bell had returned to the post which commanded the courtyard, that Hanbury asked Mansel and me to come to the staircase-turret, where Carson was keeping watch.

Admission to the turret was gained from a secondary hall, which cut the servants' quarters from the rest of the house; like the kitchen and the servants' hall, the turret had plainly survived, when the rest of the castle was burned, for it was manifestly aged and most solidly built; I imagine that of late years it had served as a back staircase to the mansion, for there was no other, and modern oil lamps were still hanging upon its walls; but it was a dark, break-neck place; the servants that had to use it must have complained bitterly. The stair was winding and two feet six inches in width: the rises of the steps were high, and their treads at their broadest point were none too broad: the latter were, of course, wedge-shaped and tapered to nothing. There was however, good handhold in the shape of a fine, deep groove cut in the outer wall and running up with the stairs. Walls, steps and all were smooth and had once shown a high polish, seldom found upon stone.

All this Hanbury showed us by the light of a torch.

"And now," said he, "here is a curious thing."

With that, he began to descend – for we had gone slowly up – and, when we were all but down, showed us a little landing, which we had scarcely observed, in the midst of the stair.

There were but two steps below it, between it and the hall, and the landing curved, as did the steps it served.

"But for this landing," said George, "the stairs would not be so steep. It's hardly a landing; it's really the third stair up – with a very broad tread; about four feet in breadth. And the height it has cost the staircase has been regained by making inconveniently high the rises of the following stairs."

When he had pointed this out, it was quite evident. "And now," he continued, "look at the hand-rail." Then he showed us that the hand-rail ceased where the landing began, and began again at once where the landing ceased.

"Finally," said Hanbury, "look at this rise."

With that, he stepped into the hall and lowered the torch.

At the top of the third rise, that is to say, two inches below the landing, were two little slots in the stone.

"*By Jove*," cried Mansel. "An *oubliette*."

"An *oubliette*," said Hanbury. "The innkeeper said there were no cellars, and I've no doubt he's right. But, if this isn't Axel the Red's superfluous guest-chamber, the next time I see him I'll walk up to Rose Noble and ask him the way to go home."

Then he showed us that the broad tread or landing was composed of four stones, three of which were slabs and could probably be withdrawn, as the lid of a pencil-box; but the fourth was fixed. Each was wedge-shaped, that is to say, it had the shape of a step.

"And now imagine," he concluded, "those three slabs withdrawn. The guest is descending in the dark. Suddenly he steps into space, and, when he clutches at the hand-rail, *the hand-rail is gone*. What sort of a fall he has *remains to be seen*."

Without a word, Mansel turned and left us, to seek some implements, while I went down on my knees and put my two forefingers into the slots. These led into two holes, cut in the broad tread, and, so soon as I felt them, I had no longer any doubt that Hanbury's conclusion was no fancy, but a substantial truth.

And so it proved.

Mansel returned with a sponge, and was quickly followed by Rowley, bearing some tools and cord.

So soon as the landing was cleansed, it was easy to discern the joints, and even the scratches, made upon the wall of the turret when the slabs had been withdrawn.

These marks were slightly higher than we should have expected to see them; but Mansel said that that showed that, before we could draw it out, we must somehow raise the edge of the first slab, for no doubt there was a fillet below, which held it locked into place.

In this he was right, and, but for his wit, we might have sought to withdraw the slab for forty days in vain; but, when we had raised no more than an eighth of an inch, by means of a wedge, it yielded at once to our efforts and came directly away without any fuss.

Here let me say that the workmanship expended upon this devilish contrivance deserved a worthier theme, for the trap was most beautifully made. Each slab was recessed upon one of its edges, flanged on the other and mitred on either side, and each lay so snug against its fellow, the turret wall and the spindle round which the staircase curled, that, as Mansel said at the time, "only a brilliant observation would have seen anything at all in the landing but clumsiness of construction."

We had now before us a hole, admitting to some dark place, so Mansel went off to recover and mend the searchlight, while Hanbury, Rowley and I withdrew the remaining slabs. When these had been displaced, the hole revealed was some three and half feet long; and of all the unfortunates who ever stepped into that space I cannot think one was saved; for, as I have said already, there was no hand-rail, the stonework around was polished, and the sides of the trap were mitred, so that even the chances of an ape that had lost its balance there would have been small indeed.

The air that came from below smelt fairly fresh and was not dank. But the darkness was impenetrable.

Presently Mansel returned, with the searchlight in working order, and, when we had made this fast, we lowered it into the hole.

The first thing its beam revealed was the "bed" upon which any victim of the trap must fall.

This was nothing less than a Cornish stile, this is to say, six low, thin fences of stone, built parallel and eighteen inches apart. As these were full forty feet below the trap, that anyone falling upon them from the staircase could fail to be broken in pieces was unthinkable. The very look of them shocked us, for it was terrible to regard preparation so nice, deliberate and permanent to send a fellow creature to meet his God. Presently Hanbury spoke.

"Let me go down," he said. "I'm not afraid of ghosts."

"I'll come with you," said I. "It's a two-men job."

When Mansel had brought the searchlight, he had brought a rope also, as well as the measuring-line. But he had not brought the seat which we had used in the well; so Rowley was sent for this and for a loose cushion, which we could use as a pad between the rope and the stone.

While he was gone, Mansel kept sniffing the air and, after a little, announced that the *oubliette* had some opening we could not see.

"I can feel no draught," he said, "but I'll swear that this air is fresh. And that's as it should be. It was sometimes advisable to empty an *oubliette*, but to use the trap for that purpose would have been inconvenient. There was, therefore, a second entrance." He stopped there to clap Hanbury on the back. "If I am right," he continued, "and such an entrance exists *on the northern or river side* – well, if George Hanbury likes to demand two thirds of the treasure as his share, I don't believe we can fairly dispute his claim."

Though I had not Mansel's foresight, I heartily agreed, for, if we had air to breathe, the dungeon was plainly the place from which to drive our shaft, and, though a vent-hole would conduct the sound of our labour, provided it gave upon the river, there would be no one to hear.

Then Rowley returned with the seat and the loose cushion, and, without more ado, Hanbury was lowered into the *oubliette*. When he was down, I followed, full of instructions from Mansel to walk delicately and, above all things, not to give tongue, "for," said he, "there is never any mistaking a voice which comes from under ground, and, if, as I think, we have found the clue to our labyrinth, it would be a thousand pities to put the enemy wise."

The dungeon was some thirty feet square and roughly walled with stones, laid in cement. The weight of the turret was taken by three tremendous piers, between two of which lay the stile; this hideous thing was built of clean-cut stone, with a low wall at either end to hold the fences in place. The piers and the stile stood in a corner of the dungeon and took up much of its room. The place did not seem very damp, but was chill and smelt of the earth. So far as we could see, the walls were everywhere sound.

All this I observed with difficulty, for Hanbury had found a doorway, before I was down, and would scarcely permit me to look around for impatience to see whither the postern led.

The doorway was barred by an old, iron gate, with a great clumsy lock, whose tongues, when shot, protruded into the stone jamb; but, though the gate was closed, it was not locked – an old negligence, I suppose, of some varlet which the Count himself might have pardoned, since the dead cannot open gates whether they be fastened or no.

The doorway admitted to a passage some five feet wide. This began at once to descend; there were no steps, but a very steep, smooth incline, upon which, such was its angle, it would have been easy to fall; but some old, iron dogs, cemented at regular intervals into the walls, afforded handhold.

We descended gingerly; Hanbury went first, and I came behind him, with the lamp in my hand.

We had gone, it seemed, a long way, when the passage ran suddenly into another chamber, not so big as the first and, though lofty, not nearly so high. Its longer wall – for it was rectangular – was before us and contained three deep embrasures, the slits of which were rudely blocked with timbers, which were barred, like shutters, into place. That these windows looked out upon the world was evident, for, so soon as we masked the searchlight, little streaks of daylight were appearing from all three: And from them, of course, came the air which had kept the great dungeon fresh.

At first it seemed that this was as far as we could go, but, after a little, we found a loose slab in a corner, close to the window wall. This was round, like a cellar pate, and might have sealed the mouth of a cistern, for a bar had been sunk in its middle, by which a strong man could lift it out of its place.

We were by now quite sure that we were in a gallery which had been cut out of the cliff and that, when the shutters were down, we should see the river below us and the road on its farther side; but, though to my mind it did not matter – for, by the embrasures, we could have plenty of air – the slab did not look to me as though it was concealing an entrance, because for one thing, it was round and, for another, too small to be hiding a flight of steps. And here I was at once right and wrong, for, when I had lifted it aside, the daylight showed us no entrance, but an exit as clean and simple as ever I saw. This was plainly a shoot, big enough to let a man's body, and leading at a very steep angle directly to the river below. It was round and smooth, like a drain, and about a third of its mouth was under water.

We discovered later that the shoot in fact discharged into a deep pool; and I think there is little doubt that the bodies of those who had died upon the stile in the *oubliette* were afterwards disposed of in this way; for a corpse had but to be loaded, head and foot, and then shot into the pool, to sink into well-nigh impregnable oblivion.

That the passage by which we had come was little more than a ramp, down which to drag a body was child's play, I think supports this view; but we never could make up our minds upon the purpose which the galley or second chamber had been constructed to serve. It may have been a dungeon; it may have been merely the dreadful "robing-room" in which the dead were "attired" for the last journey; it may have been a retreat to which the Count could withdraw, if the castle fell, where he could rest for a while before he made his escape. Be that as it may, so far as we were concerned, it was a perfect withdrawing-room, airy, secluded, safe, and actually adjoining the dungeon from which we must drive our shaft.

And that was as far as I could see.

Then we returned to the dungeon, and Hanbury ascended, and Mansel came down in his stead. I showed him all we had found. When we came to the shoot, he laughed.

"We're doomed to get wet," he said.

I did not understand, and said so.

Mansel fingered his chin.

"William," he said, "that bomb put the wind up us properly. So much so that this very night we leave Wagensburg – bag, baggage and cars – never to return. At least, that, I trust, is what Rose Noble will think. Of course, he's no fool, Rose Noble. But, if we leave the stable doors open, he'll have something to go on, won't he? And I think we might call at the inn, to say 'Goodbye' to the landlord. That would be almost artistic."

I could only stare.

Mansel laughed. Then he waved a hand at the chamber.

"Dormitory and parlour," he said, "until the treasure is won. The cars stabled at Villach; supplies delivered by night, by means of the shoot. And, when we're through, what an exit! Simple, unobtrusive and swift. All we need is a boat. Of course, George Hanbury should receive the DSO. And I think perhaps Axel the Red deserves a 'mention' ".

By noon we had lowered into the *oubliette* everything loose that we had, except, of course, some arms and the furniture of the cars. Then Mansel and Carson descended, to arrange the electric light and install a muffled bell which should ring from the mouth of the shoot.

By lunch-time all was in order, and we had but to lay our plans.

These were easy to make.

We soon decided to leave Rowley and Bell behind in the *oubliette*, while the rest of us took the cars and left for Villach. To procure a good base should be easy; but we might have to go to Salzburg to find a collapsible boat. It seemed likely that we should be back by the following night. But, before we left the castle, there remained to be done two things of some importance. The first was to see, if we could, what action the enemy was taking; and the second, *to determine, once for all, the direction in which to dig our shaft.*

Now, when I perceived the gravity of this decision, the extreme difficulty of taking it and the impossibility of verifying its accuracy, I must honestly confess that my heart failed me. Had we had the estate to ourselves, to drive a tunnel near two hundred yards in length and twenty-five feet below ground, so as to hit a chamber some six feet square, would to my mind, have been a very difficult feat; but to accomplish this without being able so much as to survey, with this idea, the surface beneath which we were to burrow, without one definite measurement upon which to found our endeavour, would be, I felt, to perform a miracle.

Indeed, I said as much; to find, to my relief, that we were not so ill-equipped as I had imagined, for it appeared that, the evening before, whilst I was in the well, Mansel had pulled out a compass and taken a bearing by which he had determined the angle at which the shaft left the well. "And that," said he, "is the kernel of the knowledge we need. The rest I will get, if not today, tomorrow, and, if not tomorrow, the next day. There's therefore, no cause for concern. Finally, we have yet to reconnoitre; and if we can wring a survey out of a reconnaissance, so much the better."

Such comfortable words, coming from Mansel, went far to rout my misgivings, but I could not help hoping very hard that some sort of survey would be made possible by the enemy's absence from the well, and at once proposed that I should go up to the roof, and, taking care to keep out of sight, see if I could perceive any sign of activity. To this suggestion Mansel agreed, and within five minutes I was upon the slates, looking towards the great well.

I could not see the meadow for the bushes and trees, but work of some sort was proceeding about the well, for, though there was no sound of the windlass, I heard repeatedly the smack of stone upon stone, and once the loose clatter of stones being shot on to the ground. These sounds I could not interpret, and since I could hear nothing else and could see nowhere any movement, I presently descended to the hall and made my report.

That the thieves were drawing no water delighted us all, for nothing could have shown us more plainly how much they were underrating the activity of the springs. Moreover, by their failure to bail, they were throwing away the precious fruit of our labour, and, of their ignorance, letting slip an invaluable advantage. When we had first taken possession, some fifty-five feet of water had covered the mouth of the shaft; at day break this morning it was hidden by, at the most, nineteen; but, if they did not begin bailing before dawn on the following day, the water would by then have regained almost the whole of the ground we had been at such pains to capture.

"Which shows," said Hanbury, "that the innkeeper isn't with them. If he were, he'd have put them wise."

"Don't be too sure," said Mansel. "It's a hundred to one they wouldn't take his advice: but what is still more likely is that he'll hold his tongue. He doesn't want to help Rose Noble to the treasure. What would be his reward? Why, as like as not, they'd leave him down in the well. He knows that perfectly. And that's why I very much hope they have impressed him. It will keep him out of mischief, and the quality of help he'll give them will do as much harm as good."

It was then arranged that he and I and Carson should go out on patrol, while Rowley watched the courtyard, and Hanbury and Bell covered our advance from the other side of the house.

Carson was to start from the courtyard, pass through the great gateway and move towards the meadow, with the path on his left; Mansel and I were to start from the West of the mansion; and we went to meet, if we could, in a dip which lay between the meadow and the trees which sheltered the house.

Before we set out, we closed the mouth of the dungeon. Then we took a pistol apiece; and Mansel put in his pocket a compass and a measuring-tape.

"And please remember," he said, "we're not out to fight; we're going to see what's afoot and to mark the lie of the land: a fuss, therefore, means failure; if there's anyone in our way we must wait till he moves: he's sure to do that before sundown, and it's only just two. And there's the slogan for today: 'Take your time.' "

Mansel and I could only emerge from a window upon the first floor, for all those below were barred; but we had a short rope-ladder, which we had not yet tried. This certainly served our purpose, but it was the most awkward appliance I ever have used, for its rungs were of rope and gave way beneath my weight in a most disconcerting manner.

When we were down, Hanbury drew up the ladder, leaving only a little grey cord to hang against the wall, some seven feet above ground. We had but to twitch this to bring down the ladder at once; so, though it was very improbable that an unfriendly eye would perceive anything suspicious, our means of ascent was continually assured.

The first thing we did was to gain the shelter of the trees and lie down in the long grass. There we lay for ten minutes as still as death. During all that time we heard not the faintest sound, except, very indistinctly, the stony clink and clatter which I had heard from the roof.

At length Mansel gave the signal, and we began to move.

Using the greatest caution, we crawled South, keeping as close to the castle as the covert allowed. So we came to the corner where the staircase-turret stood. Here, again, we lay still for ten minutes or more. Then Mansel rose to his knees, and from his knees to his feet. For a moment he stood like a statue; then he looked slowly around. The next instant he was at the base of the turret, measuring-tape in hand.

I do not think that anything I ever saw Mansel do impressed me so much as the little survey he made at the foot of the castle wall. He was full in the open, and against the white, sunlit stone he offered a perfect mark; the work he was doing, if seen, would as good as betray our plans; his nearest cover was twenty-five paces away. Yet, though he worked for six minutes, he never once looked about him or even raised his head. Swiftly and silently he used the compass and tape, going about his business with the deliberate precision of one to whom time is no object, and entering figures in a notebook, as though he had the world to himself.

When he was quite finished, he took a long nail from his pocket and, placing its point where he had made a slight mark, pressed it well into the ground; then he hooked the end of the tape upon the head of the nail, and stepped across to where I lay in the grass.

"Kneel for a minute," he said. I knelt. "You see that fir to our left, with the broken bough like a spout? I'm going to measure exactly how far it stands from the nail. Follow me, with the tape in your hand. Hold it continually taut, so that whatever happens it doesn't slip off the nail."

With that, he lay down in the grass and began to steal forward, paying out the tape as he went.

We had crawled and lain still and crawled again for nearly half an hour, and, so much were my fingers aching, I was beginning to wish the treasure at the bottom of the sea, when Mansel turned his head and signed to me to come alongside.

"I can smell tobacco," he breathed.

We were still ten paces from the fir, to which, except for the bushes, we had had a clear run: in threading the tape through these, Mansel had shown infinite patience, for, as may be readily understood, it was a trying exercise, and to perform it noiselessly had entailed a lot of finical labour.

At first I could smell no smoke, but after a moment or two a whiff came to my nose, and I was immediately sure that it came from the South. I told Mansel this, whereupon he at once went forward, bidding me to stay where I was. Half a length clear of me he stopped, and, after a long wait, signed for me to come on. When I had done so and was lying alongside, he told me very gently to part the grass.

The first thing I saw was that we were at the end of the covert through which we had crawled and that the fir stood clear, on the edge of the little dip where we were to join Carson. Beyond lay the meadow. In this, twenty paces away, stood a little, curved breastwork composed of flat, loose stones such as go to the making of piled walls, and built to shelter a sentry from every side but the South. This little sconce was occupied, for the smoke we had smelt was floating over its parapet, and the crown of a soft, felt hat was just to be seen. Whoever was there was plainly taking his ease and was sitting down on the ground, with his back to the wall.

In the distance, about the well, Rose Noble was directing the building of a kind of redoubt, in the shape of a wall of flat stones piled one upon the other and packed together with earth. These were brought up from the combe, from some wall or cabin, I suppose, which we had not observed, and were borne on a sort of hurdle by a bearer at either end. The sun was hot, and I did not envy them their labour; and, indeed, it was very clear that they did not like it themselves, for they staggered under their loads, like drunken men, and finally discharged them with the slovenly recklessness of one who is past caring.

Some sort of system was observed, for the two that had brought up the stones packed those they had brought into place, while the others reluctantly descended in search of more: but, partly for want of stones and partly because of the laziness of its builders, which was quite laughable to watch, the wall rose very slowly, and I was not surprised to see Rose Noble fiercely impatient of such half-heartedness. What he said I could not hear, but the contempt and indignation of his gestures were unmistakable.

Perhaps, for us, the most engaging sight was that of the landlord of the inn, his wrist fastened by a cord to that of Punter, taking his turn with the latter of bringing up stones on the hurdle and packing them into place. A more dejected-looking workman I never have seen, and I imagine he was cursing the treasure and the well and Wagensburg from the bottom of his heart.

No one of them was suitably attired for manual labour, but Job was wearing a pair of white flannel trousers, which might have afforded him comfort, had he not been so anxious to keep them clean. In this the labour was against him, and his manifest concern for their condition was constantly provoking Rose Noble's wrath.

Ellis was not to be seen, which satisfied us that he was behind the breastwork, performing the duties of a sentinel according to his lights.

Now, all this encouraged me greatly, and, I fancy, Mansel as well; for it was plain as a pikestaff that, though the thieves "meant business," when they felt the pinch of labour there was only one man among them worth his salt, and that, if they could not draw water any better than they could build walls, their chances of reaching the shaft were slight indeed, to say nothing of Ellis' exhibition, for which he deserved to be shot. All the same, there were still six paces between us and the fir, which was our immediate goal, and these lay in view of the meadow and all its occupants.

Now this, though I did not then know it, did not matter at all, for what Mansel had wanted to do was to reach some point from which he could see the well. And this we had done. So, after a little, he brought out a second nail and pressed it into the ground. The distance between the two nails was eighty-one yards. He then took the bearing of the well from the second nail. When he had done this, for an hour he lay very still, like a dog, with his eyes fixed upon the meadow and his chin on his hands. He told me later that during that time he endured the torment of a thief who, holding already some earring of very great value, regards its fellow from without some jeweller's shop; for that, having got so far, not to be able to measure the distance from where we lay to the well was exasperating indeed.

At last he whispered to me to move a few paces back towards the house and to wait for him in a place where the cover was thick.

I had hardly done so before I saw Carson's head a little way to our left, and, so soon as he saw that I saw him, he nodded and disappeared.

As soon as Mansel was back, he spoke in my ear.

"I think we must make a bid for the distance from the covert to the well. We may not need it; but, if we don't take it now, I don't think we shall be able to take it at all. Unless I'm mistaken, they're not only building a shelter; *they're building their future home*; and the idea of surveying even the curtilage of Rose Noble's bower, when occupied, makes no appeal to me. Now to drive them out of the meadow, would be of no use; they'd certainly run for shelter, but, as soon as they'd won it, they'd stand; and then, though they might not hurt us, they'd see us at work. And that would be fatal. The only thing to be done is to draw them into the combe. Please, therefore, go back and get Hanbury. Leave the house together and see that Bell or Rowley pulls up the ladder out of sight. Then make your way to the combe, bearing West, well away from the meadow, beyond the sentinel peak. Locate their depot of stones and try to pick up their car. Then decide two things – first, what feint is most likely to draw them into the combe, and, secondly, how you and Hanbury are going to retire on the house. When you've taken these two decisions, await a convenient moment, and then demonstrate. Fire, start the engine of the car, shout – according as you think best. If you can do it, I should think the car is a sure draw. And the moment you've got them going, fade right away. For heaven's sake take no risks; it isn't worth it. And a minute and a half is enough for Carson and me. Now, is all that clear?"

I nodded.

"Good," breathed Mansel. "As you go, please release the tape and pocket the nail; and remember, *take your time*."

"I will," I said.

Then I turned and left him, and started to crawl back towards the house.

It was, I suppose, some thirty minutes later that Hanbury and I rounded the south-western shoulder of the sentinel peak to see the closed car below us on a grass-grown track, close to a ruinous byre. Of this the walls were standing, and had been rudely loop-holed; but the roof was gone. Still, the place made a good blockhouse, and the ground about it was clear, affording a field of fire. The track was wet and muddy, because of all the water which we had drawn from the well; and further East, the ground to the North of the track had the look of a bog. Two or three blankets were lying spread out in the sun, and bottles and papers and tins made a disorderly litter about the spot. A door of the car was open, and on this hung somebody's coat; a couple of empty glasses stood on the running-board.

We had just observed all this when Punter and the innkeeper came plodding into view, the latter dragging the hurdle, as though he were tired of life. Arrived at the byre, Punter lay down on the ground, while the other began to pluck some stones from what was left of a pen at the side of the byre. He worked slowly enough in all conscience, yet too fast, I suppose, for Punter, for, when the hurdle was laden, the latter stared upon its burden and then, as though the sight shocked him, covered his eyes and lay back upon the ground. Indeed, so ludicrous was his demeanour that Hanbury and I began to shake with laughter, and, when his unfortunate companion began to gesticulate in manifest apprehension of the trouncing this delay would provoke, we could have roared with mirth. Punter, however, took no notice at all, and at last the other sat down and put his head in his hands.

Before they moved again, our plans were laid.

From what we remembered of the combe, there would come a moment when Punter, mounting the slope, could see Rose Noble, yet have the car in his eye. At that moment we were to sally upon the car. I was to start her engine and, as though by accident, sound the electric horn, while Hanbury was to attack her petrol-tank. Directly we heard the cries sure to be raised we were to fire at random, and I was to run up the track and Hanbury down. Once out of sight we were to take to the woods and make our way back to the castle, I by way of the shrine and Hanbury, who was fleeter of foot, by the line we had come.

The plan was simple enough, and, I think, sound; in fact, as I shall presently show, it served its purpose; but this it did at a price which we did not expect to pay, for I had just started the engine, after sounding the horn, and was watching Punter's frenzy upon the brow of the rise, when two hands closed upon my windpipe with a grip so savage that I was unable to breathe, much less utter a sound. Be sure I fought like a madman, but the man behind me was strong and had the advantage. His thumbs were braced against the back of my neck, which might have been in a vice, and, having once got such a hold, for him to prevent me from leaving the driver's seat was very easy. It seemed a long time before I heard cries raised, and then the noise of a shot. This sounded faint, and blurred, for the blood was pounding in my head, and I knew I was losing consciousness. Then I heard more cries, which seemed confused and distant, and I was still trying to determine what they might mean, when my senses left me.

"What do you know?" said Rose Noble.

I was sitting up on the ground, with my back to the near fore wheel of the closed car. The hub-cap was hurting abominably, but about this I could do nothing, because I was lashed to the spokes and could not move. Rose Noble was sitting on a box a few feet away, and, immediately opposite me, Ellis was leaning against the jamb of a doorway, framed by a high stone wall, with a cigar in his mouth. For a moment or two I could not make out where I was; then I saw that the car had been moved to the farther side of the byre, which now stood between me and the combe, and wholly concealed it from anyone North of the track.

I must have lain unconscious a long time, for the sun had just gone down.

"What do you know?" said Rose Noble.

"I refuse to talk," said I, "until you loosen this cord. I expect to be tied up, but this hub-cap is breaking my back."

Ellis laughed and spat, but Rose Noble only regarded me, rubbing his nose. Then, to my surprise, he rose and, coming behind me, began to loosen my bonds. Ellis' surprise was plainly greater than mine, for, when he saw Rose Noble's purpose, he started forward with an oath, and dropped his cigar.

"What the devil are you doing?" he cried.

The other told him not to be a fool.

When the strain was gone, I thanked him, and he made fast the cords.

"And now," he said, resuming his seat in the box, "what do you know?"

"I believe," said I, "there's a chamber at the bottom of that well."

"How far down?" said Rose Noble.

"Most of the way," said I. "I can't tell you for certain, because there was still too much water when I last went down; but I think it lies pretty low."

"Were you the last to go down?"

"I was."

"Can you speak German?" said Rose Noble.

"Not a word."

I knew what was in his mind, and was glad to make a true answer, for to lie when your statement cannot be checked is one thing, but to give a reply which another captive may instantly show to be false is another matter.

"When you say 'chamber,' " said Rose Noble, "what do you mean?"

I told him of the well-digger's statement, only omitting to speak any word of the shaft.

"Then the treasure's under water?" he said.

"It must be," said I. "In some recess in the wall."

"How far down did you get?"

"About forty feet below high-water mark."

"That tells me nothing," said Rose Noble. "How close did you get to the bottom of the well?"

"Within twenty-five feet."

The man's bearing was curiously soft; he was certainly examining me, but his manner was not unpleasant, though something abrupt; all the time he kept his eyes on my face, tilting his chin a little and blinking musingly.

"And now," he said, looking away, "what are your plans?"

"At the present moment," said I, "we have no plans."

For a moment Rose Noble did not move. Then he looked round and upon me, with his eyes wide.

I have tried before to describe the horror these lent his countenance, but I do not think I can ever begin to convey the appalling malevolence of his terrible gaze. It was not human; and, as I met it, I felt my hair rise upon my head.

"Guess again," he purred.

I made him no answer, partly because I dared not trust my voice.

"Mansel," continued Rose Noble, "sent you two guys down here, to draw us away from the well. Why?"

I was so much confounded by the man's discernment that, instead of directly traversing what can only have been a conjecture, dressed up as a fact, I said nothing at all, but only stared upon him like a man in a dream.

"Why?"

I swallowed with difficulty.

"Mansel doesn't talk," I said hoarsely, "even to me. I know he wanted to have a look at the well, but he didn't say why."

The eyes seemed to scorch my brain.

"Why d'you think?"

I could only shake my head.

"He's lying," said Ellis. "He knows."

"Yes," said Rose Noble. "He knows." He raised his voice. "Bunch!" The driver of the car appeared. "Take off the fan-strap."

I suppose I might have known what was coming, but not until the belt had been taken from the cooling-fan it controlled and I had been spread-eagled, with my back flat against the radiator of the car, did I realize that pressure in the shape of heat was to be put upon me to open my mouth. I had but a shirt to my back, and I could feel that the radiator was just warm.

"Start her up," said Rose Noble.

Bunch started the engine: then he played with the throttle, until she was "idling" in a leisurely way.

Rose Noble got to his feet.

"I am not in the habit," he said, "of wasting my time. I shall, therefore, require your answer *before* you are taken down. Bear that in mind. *Before*. So don't wait too long before announcing your readiness to reply. Leave, so to speak, a margin of endurance."

The cold, imperious tone stung me to speech.

"That's not the way," said I, "to address your betters."

Ellis, who was moving away, stopped in his stride and turned: Bunch, who was fastening a bootlace, looked up at me, open-mouthed: Rose Noble stood very still.

At length: "That was a mistake," he said slowly, "which Mansel would never have made."

"Very likely," said I, for I saw I had drawn blood, and this exhilarated me. "But then, he's enough brain for five. And isn't he quick with his hands?"

Rose Noble lifted his head and looked at the sky. This was dark with clouds, coming up from the West.

"After all," he said, as though in soliloquy, "swans sing, don't they? So why not a cygnet?"

Then he turned and walked firmly away, passing out of sight round the byre; Ellis followed him; and presently Rose Noble's voice called Bunch, and I was left alone.

It was more than half dark now, and already the radiator was growing unpleasantly warm. I attempted to hollow my back, but I was lashed so tight that I could only spare one region at the expense of another. I, therefore, began an endeavour to stretch the cords; unless I could do this quickly, I should not be able, I knew, to do it at all, for to brace myself against the radiator would soon be out of the question. I, therefore, like Samson, put forth all my strength, taking the strain for a quarter of a minute at a time, with the happy result that, after three or four efforts, though the cords held, I must have added full half an inch to their length, for I was able to stand quite clear of the now fiery metal. This was a great relief, but I knew that, unless I was soon to be saved, I had but postponed my torment.

I have often wondered why I did not lose heart, for my plight was really desperate, and my rescue could only follow the very capture of the byre; but, I suppose, a merciful Providence

DORNFORD YATES

heartens those who else would have no hope at all, so that they may not be called upon to bear too great a burden. So I stood there hopefully, with my eyes on the corner of the byre, listening for any sound.

Suddenly a shot rang out.

Ellis was the first to appear, whipping into safety, like the dastard he was; Rose Noble and Bunch followed hastily enough. They all passed into the byre without a word.

After a moment or two: "That was Job's side," said Ellis. "Why doesn't the — come in?"

"Because he's asleep," sneered Rose Noble. "That's the only thing that would keep Job at his post."

Then I heard two more shots, and almost at once Bunch cried: "There he is by the rotten stump. I can see his pants."

Here came another shot, and those in the byre cried out that Job was down.

"Serve him right," said Rose Noble, "for showing them where to shoot. This isn't Wimbledon."

"He's up," cried Bunch. "He's up. Punched, though. Lame as a — tree."

"What did I say?" said Rose Noble. And then, with a dirty oath, "He'd be something more than lame if I'd been behind him."

Here came the scuttle of feet, and Punter rounded the byre and flashed within.

"Job's stopped one," he cried, panting.

"You might teach him to run," said Rose Noble, acidly. "Take the right wall."

"Curse this dark," said Ellis. "I can't see a — thing."

"There's nothing to see," said Rose Noble. "We've only got to sit tight an' – "

"He's down again," cried Bunch. "Crawlin' in."

"Oh, — Job," said Rose Noble. "Crawling or lying, what the hell do we care? Time to – "

108

A little burst of fire drowned what else he was saying, and I heard a bullet strike upon stone, and another sing over my head.

"Three flashes in front," said Rose Noble. "Now for the other two."

As though in reply came two shots, not far away.

"Five," said Rose Noble. "Thank you, you clumsy fools. Ellis, they're under that hump, trying to move around. Keep your eye on the track: they can't cross that unseen. Bunch, take the left with Ellis and watch that road."

"Job coming up, Punter," said Bunch. "Don' – "

The profane unanimity with which his companions consigned poor Job and all his works to the devil argued that they had slight use for a wounded man. Had it been Ellis or Rose Noble, I do not think the others would have been any more concerned; for they were confederates of necessity, and not at all of choice.

There was another spurt of shots.

"Three from the hump," said Ellis. "An' they don't fancy that road."

"Show you can see it," said Rose Noble, "just to encourage the swine."

As Ellis fired, Job crawled round the edge of the byre into my view, trailing his left leg. When he was round, he stopped short of the doorway, as though he had done enough. After a little, he propped himself on an elbow and looked about him.

The firing was hotter now, and, once and again, Ellis fired down the road. He or Rose Noble always counted the flashes in a loud voice.

Job had seen me and was plainly puzzled by my attitude, for he craned his neck and peered, like a dim-sighted man. But even this inspection did not apparently satisfy his curiosity, for, after a little, he fell again upon his face and started to drag himself painfully almost up to my feet. There he lay for a moment, as though the effort had been too much for him. Then his arms stole out, and *I felt him cutting my bonds.*

"One flash from the right," said Rose Noble. "Punter, watch your road."

"Three from the hump," said Ellis, and fired again.

"Can you walk?" breathed Mansel.

"Yes," said I, free and trembling.

"Follow me."

He stepped out of sight of the doorway behind the car, with me in his wake. Then he put his hand under my arm, and we began to run. A hundred yards later he stopped, to rip Job's trousers from his legs. Then we crossed the track and headed straight for the combe. Half-way up this, Mansel drew his pistol and, standing with his back to the byre, fired four shots in succession into the air.

"That's the rally," he explained. "And now you get back to the house. The courtyard door is open. And you might give Tester some water and tell him that I shall be back in a quarter of an hour."

Mansel was as good as his word, and twenty-five minutes later we were all six within doors.

If I had then expected to hear his tale, I was disappointed, for Carson was sent forthwith to prepare the cars, and Rowley and Bell made ready to enter the *oubliette*.

Bell was the older of the two, and Mansel put him in charge.

"Move very carefully," he said, "and make no unnecessary noise. During the day you may take down one of the shutters and open the shoot. You may do the same by night, provided you show no light. If I don't come tomorrow night, I shall come the next night without fail; but not, of course, during the day. The bell from the shoot is muffled, so sleep with it to your ear; and test it at dusk."

Then we lowered them into the dungeon, and, when they had found the searchlight, we slid the slabs back into place.

Mansel oversaw this action, himself wiping every edge with great particularity; and, when it was done, he took a handful of dust, which he had got from some chamber, and sprinkled it over the landing from side to side. Then he took a cloth and smeared the dust to and fro, finally wiping it off into an empty tin. When he had done this, not a joint was visible.

Much of the ceiling of the hall which led to the turret had been brought down by the bomb, and the powder had floated up the staircase and settled on every tread. That we had been busy hereabouts was, therefore, most evident, for the stairs were covered with footprints, especially about the mouth of the *oubliette*. We, therefore, swept the staircase as far as the windows we had used, after which Mansel took off his shoes and powdered it over again by dashing a bag full of plaster against the wall. We then pulled down most of the remains of the ceiling, to cover our use of the hall, and, when all the powder had settled, Hanbury and I walked once up and down the stairs.

So soon as this was done, we repaired to the stables, and, whilst Hanbury kept watch in the gateway, Mansel and Carson and I man-handled the cars through the courtyard on to the road of approach. When we felt them moving under their own weight, we put on the brakes. The Rolls was in rear.

Then Mansel closed the stables and left by the kitchen hall door, locking it behind him; and, a moment later, we were moving down the drive in silence, except for the creak of leather and the brush of the tyres.

Hanbury and Carson rode in the first car, and Mansel, Tester and I went in the Rolls. When we came to the first bend, Mansel switched on our lights.

Lest someone of the village should notice that we were but four, Hanbury and Carson were to thread it as fast as they could, while Mansel and I were to stop and call at the inn.

This we did, to find the innkeeper's wife in an uneasy temper, for, said she, her husband had gone out at dusk the day before, but had not said whither he was going, and had not returned. She rather feared, she added, that he was gone after some gypsies who always passed through Carinthia at this time of the year, and sometimes had with them horses which they were too ready to sell below their market worth. Mansel shrugged his shoulders and paid our account. When the woman asked if we were going, he said we should be back in ten days.

With that, we left her standing in the mouth of the inn, and, presently overtaking the others, reached Villach within the hour.

And there, whilst we ate our supper, Mansel told me his tale.

"I measured the distance," he said, "from the second nail to the well. I made sure we should rouse friend Ellis behind the breastwork, but Carson had him covered, so I counted him out. The distance was one hundred and eleven yards. I sank the three buckets and I cut the two pulleys adrift and let them fall. Then, for the first time, I glanced at the sconce. *It was empty*, except for a hat on the top of a stick. By the side of the stick was a brazier, made out of a tin, and a handful of tobacco on some charcoal was smouldering gently. Not a very elaborate device, but, as no doubt Rose Noble surmised, quite good enough to fool me.

"I confess that I felt humiliated, but I was much more alarmed. I had sent you down to play with an empty car – not to take tea with Ellis, who, you were sure, was asleep a quarter of a mile away.

"I reached the edge of the wood, to the right of the combe, in time to see the car being backed out of sight behind the byre. You were lying on the ground – to my great relief no worse than senseless, for Ellis was lashing your wrists behind your back. Then he and Bunch picked you up and lugged you behind the byre. I observed that this had been loop-holed.

"It was clear that nothing could be usefully done towards your rescue until the sun was down and you had regained consciousness; so I left Carson to watch and returned for reinforcements. Hanbury, of course, believed you half-way to the shrine. While I was gone, Job and Punter were posted on either side of the combe. The landlord was tied to a tree – I suppose, for the night. Job went to sleep, of course; and, for the second time, Carson laid him out. It was then that I had the idea of assuming his personality. I pretended a wound, of course, to cover my limp; to tire and crawl in was the corollary of the wound. But I never hoped to find you without the byre."

When I tried to say I was grateful, he would have none of my thanks.

"Had I been in your case," he said shortly, "you would have done the same."

For all that, to go down alone to that byre was a brave thing to do; and I think the knowledge that discovery would almost inevitably entail a fate far more dreadful than any sudden death would have daunted most men I know.

6

Tester Gives Tongue

We established three bases – one at Salzburg, another at an inn at Villach, and the third at the village at which Mansel and Carson and I had lain on our way to Wagensburg. The name of this village was St Martin, and it was distant from Lerai some thirty-five miles.

One base would have been enough; but three made our path smooth, for, by their use, curiosity regarding our movements was, so to speak, still-born, and an ample supply of fresh food was continually assured.

Had we but one base, the employment of a car *by night only*, the regular disappearance and return of the reliefs into which we were divided, and the constant demand for food to victual six men must have excited comment; but, as I shall show, the use of three bases altogether concealed our business, suggested that our party was consisting of but two men and argued nothing more eccentric than a zealous interest in exploring the countryside.

It was early decided that we should labour in pairs and that of every three days each pair should pass forty-eight hours in the dungeon and twenty-four hours abroad. Each pair was to have its own base, to which it alone would repair, and, the second car having been bestowed at Salzburg, only the Rolls would be employed.

Mansel and Carson were to use Salzburg: Hanbury and Rowley, Villach; Bell and I, St Martin.

By way of illustration, Bell and I would leave St Martin on a Monday evening, ostensibly to tour the country, taking sufficient food to last us for two full days. That night we would enter the dungeon, and Hanbury and Rowley would leave. Now, two days' provision for two is one day's provision for four, so that the food we had brought would feed Mansel, Carson, Bell and myself on Tuesday, and on Tuesday night Hanbury and Rowley would be back with a fresh supply. Upon their arrival, Mansel and Carson would leave, returning on Wednesday night to relieve myself and Bell.

This system worked very well; and I am sure that not one of our respective landlords so much as suspected the tale which, had it had a tongue, the Rolls could have told.

The establishment of the bases, the bestowal of the second car, and the discovery and purchase of a collapsible boat took more than one day to accomplish; and forty-eight hours had gone by before Mansel, Hanbury, Carson and I alighted finally from the Rolls, two hundred yards from the river, and a little to the West of the bend above which the castle stood. The river was flowing from West to East, so we were up stream.

The night was fine, still, and very dark. For the last three miles we had travelled without any lights; but the inhabitants of Carinthia go early to bed, and we had met no one.

A hiding-place for the car was easy to find, and a little old quarry, long abandoned to Nature and approached by a grass-grown track, suited our purpose admirably. And here, in the thick of some bushes, we arranged to conceal the boat,

Then Mansel made much of Tester and set him to guard the car, telling him in so many words that Hanbury would return in two days' time. I am sure that the dog understood for all his sprightliness left him, and he whimpered a little, when Mansel turned away. Carson told me later that that was his way; and I can testify to his indifference, when I brought him to meet Hanbury, and Hanbury to his excitement when he brought him to meet his lord.

Then we took up the boat and her sculls and the tools and the food we had brought, and went down to the river.

This was smooth-flowing, and the current was slight. After a short search we found a convenient place, where a tree overhung deep water and a man could take hold of a branch and lower himself with ease into a boat below. Here it was simple, too, to launch the boat, which was astonishingly light; and Mansel, Carson and I were soon aboard. The boat would hold but three, and since Hanbury and Rowley were to lie that night at Villach, the former stayed where he was.

Three minutes later we were at the mouth of the shoot, and Mansel put up a hand and rang the bell. At once the flap was lifted, and I heard Bell asking if he should show a light.

"On no account," said Mansel. "But let the rope ladder down."

It must have been near half an hour before we stood in the gallery, for this was, of course, the first time we had used the shoot, and, since, as I have said, a third of its mouth was under water, its passage required some care, unless our clothes and victuals were to be immersed. Indeed, to go up or down we always stripped to the skin. The provisions we saved by the use of a large iron bucket, with a tight-fitting lid; when we had loaded this, we spread it with oiled silk before replacing the lid; so far as I can remember, no water ever circumvented this rude device. Our clothes were raised and lowered in a waterproof sheet. After a while we grew expert, and the relief then came to be done with a soldierly dispatch.

The first thing we did was to give Rowley his instructions and pack him off. Mansel was none too easy at letting him go alone, but he said that he was a swimmer, and knew how to pull an oar, and, since the sculls were so fastened that they could not leave the boat, it seemed certain that he would come safely to the other side.

"All the same," said Mansel, "you must give us a sign, and, as I'm afraid to let you show a light, you must take this cord. Fasten it to the painter, and, when you've found Mr Hanbury, cast it off. But, before you do that, tie two knots at its end. So soon as we find it slack, we shall pull it in: and, if the knots are there, we shall know that you're safe."

With that, we put out the light and opened the shoot, and, five minutes later, two knots at the end of the cord told us that Rowley and his master had joined forces.

Bell had nothing to report; but he and Rowley had ordered all our stuff so conveniently that, without more ado, we were able to go to bed.

The next morning the new work was begun.

Mansel and Carson had bathed before I was awake, and, by the time I was ready, the measurements had been taken, and everything was in train.

Precisely at five o'clock I cut the first stone out of the dungeon wall; and, before half an hour had gone by, we had made a rectangular breach, three feet by nine feet high. To these dimensions we adhered, for, though such a height was uncalled for, it allowed the swing of a pickaxe and so paid for its maintenance many times over. To our relief, the soil behind proved sandy and so easy to work: but this condition convinced us that, as we drove our tunnel, so we must prop its roof and retain its walls with timber against a subsidence or bulge. To do this was simple, but how to produce the timber I could not think; yet Mansel had found out a way within the hour.

Some ten miles away stood a saw-mill; and there was plenty of wood such as would suit us well. Of this Mansel proposed to purchase a stack and to drive as hard a bargain as ever he could.

He would then require its free delivery to Wagensburg, "at which," said he, "the miller will certainly kick, for to carry a load of timber up that road of approach would make Hercules scratch his head. After an argument, we shall come to a compromise. I shall pay nothing for delivery, and he will dump the wood in the quarry where we stable the car. Thence, with a very ill grace, I shall consent to fetch it, as and when it is required."

And so it fell out; so that in two days' time we had ready to hand a great store of wood, of which few knew and none, I think, thought anything.

For the time being, however, we were hard put to it to find so much as a makeshift to stay the roof of the shaft; but, after a little, we sawed in pieces some benches, which we had found in the kitchen, and two days before had lowered into the *oubliette*; with their wood and that of some cases which had contained supplies, we contrived such temporary props as made it safe to proceed.

The soil we displaced we cast into the great dungeon, piling it up by the walls, for, though we must presently empty our winnings out of the shoot, to set ourselves this task before our time would have been unprofitable.

The work went apace, for we were strong men and determined, and laboured faithfully by shifts, so that the most was made of our endurance. There was plenty of air, and the conditions were, I imagine, much more pleasant than such as usually govern work below ground, for the dungeon was cool and spacious, and the second chamber made an admirable lounge.

Although we knew our direction, we were less sure of our relation to the chamber, so far as depth was concerned; but, after consultation, we decided to keep the floor of our shaft fifteen feet above that of the *oubliette*, for the meadow lay higher than the kitchen by at least five feet, and, with another nine feet – that is to say, the height of our tunnel – to correct any vertical error, we surely could not go wrong. We, therefore, drove the shaft to this level, and kept it faithfully there up to the very end. By using the compass, we checked our direction as we went, taking the bearing at least twice in the day, to avoid waste of labour.

It had been arranged that Bell and I should leave when Hanbury and Rowley returned, but our need of timber was so pressing that Carson and Mansel, who alone could deal with the miller, left in our stead. So Bell lay four nights in succession in the second chamber. This order, once taken, it seemed convenient to preserve; and, therefore, Hanbury always relieved Mansel, Mansel me, and I Hanbury.

Because his base was at Salzburg, Mansel had much less leisure than Hanbury or I; for not only was Salzburg more distant than either St Martin or Villach, but such odd things as we needed were better to be found in that town, so that duties of one sort or another were constantly imposing upon his time of rest. But, if ever we pointed this out, he would not listen, maintaining that he did very well and enjoyed any sort of occupation better than idleness.

Of the first day's labour there is no more to tell than of that of any other; and, since driving a shaft is a dull business, I shall not set down our progress, but only continue – as I have already begun, though something, I fear, at haphazard – to record such details as I think may illumine, as a picture a tale, the dry fact of our long labour; as well our odd doubts and difficulties, and the means we devised to lay them, as the happenings which stand clean out of the next six weeks and have little or nothing to do with our main endeavour; this was, in so many words, to reach the treasure-chamber before the thieves.

Our constant fear was that we should strike rock, for with that we knew very well we could not reckon, and to try to surmount such an obstacle would be work forlorn. Indeed, for a long time, whenever the pick struck a stone which was uncommonly obstinate, our hearts went into our mouths for fear that we had encountered this dreadful enemy; but, though more than once the size and rigidity of some boulder as good as realized our fears, we were spared this terrible blow, and never met anything worse than a long course of clay which later gave way to gravel as suddenly as it had taken its place.

We bathed morning and evening by way of the shoot; and, since we had no means of drying our towels, the relief always brought some fresh ones to carry it through its term. Our linen, of course, we could change when we went to the base. Indeed, all things considered, we were very well found and suffered next to no discomfort. The pavement of the gallery, certainly, made a hard bed; but, after a full day's labour, I think any one of us could have slumbered upon the stile itself.

Examining this hideous death-bed, while they were yet alone, Rowley and Bell had found two naked poniards lying between the fences and covered with dust. The hilt of one was golden and very well done; the other's was of silver and plainly made. I think there is little doubt that they had belonged to two victims, who were wearing them when they fell; and that the shock of the falls had shaken them out of their scabbards and down, clear of the bodies which they had lately adorned.

Though I never found the work irksome, I enjoyed my nights at St Martin and my days in the open air. Upon these I had seldom anything to do except to take my ease; for, as I have said, Salzburg could best supply such needs as we had, and Mansel and Carson always cared for the Rolls. By Mansel's advice, I took to trout fishing, for that was a quiet engagement and rested the body and soul; and many a pleasant hour I passed beside some comfortable stream, gaining more refreshment than fish, of which I took very few, whilst Bell and Tester went rambling somewhere within call, like children let out of school, revelling in the mysteries of wood and meadow, and turning idleness into an enterprise.

The weather was wonderfully fine; though sometimes rain fell, the fall was always heavy and soon passed, and I do not remember one day that was overcast or unseasonable.

A storm burst one night whilst the relief was taking place, or, to be more precise, when Mansel and Carson were sculling to the mouth of the shoot. Quick as we were, before they stood in the gallery their clothes were wet through; but, though the downpour was frightful, Bell and I dared not delay, lest the boat should be swamped. I never stripped more reluctantly, and even the river seemed snug beside the nakedness of the boat. The rain lashed my bare skin, whilst I sat waiting for Bell, but, when he came down and laid hold of the gunwale, as usual, to come aboard, of my endeavour to trim the craft, I slipped on the dripping thwart and fell clean into the river, capsizing the boat as I went. Meantime, unaware of this misadventure, those in the gallery let down our clothes with a run, and, believing that we had the bundle, lowered it into the water before they found out their mistake. However, we took no hurt, nor even cold in spite of our thirty-mile drive, which shows, I think, that we were in very good condition.

The searchlight consumed much power; so when Mansel left for Salzburg, he always took with him one battery and brought back another charged.

Our wireless set afforded us great pleasure. We received the English stations very well and so heard the news every evening, and music, whenever we pleased; but I fancy those that made it little dreamed that their notes were larding the shadows of so sinister a place.

That the dungeon and the chamber made up a grim suite cannot be denied; and, though no one of us said such a thing, I think we could all have spared the grisly memories with which the spot seemed charged. We were too tired to dream; what dreadful matters might else have ridden our slumbers! We laboured upon a scaffold and took our rest in a morgue: we came and went the way dead men had gone – surely, "such stuff as dreams are made on," ill dreams. But, happily for us, we were too tired to dream. Still, if some tales may be believed, not every weary man has been so favoured. Indeed, if the pitiful dead walk, they must have picked their way between us as we lay in the gallery of nights; but, perhaps because we were so sorry for them, and found their murder so detestable, they had compassion on the strangers within their gates.

So the days went by, and we drove the shaft forward, propping it with timbers as we went.

We had laboured for more than a week, before we went out to see how the thieves were faring. We were all impatient to know what things were happening in the enemy's camp, but, as Mansel said at the time, we knew far better than they that for the moment the treasure was out of their reach, and to gratify pure curiosity at the expense of our work would have been the way of a schoolgirl. "All the same," he continued, "we mustn't behave as though they had thrown in their hand; and, when they've had time to find out that they are no match for the springs and that *without assistance* they will not lower the water as far as the shaft, that will be the moment at which to begin to watch. If you must know what another is going to do, when he will not tell you and your chances of observation are limited, the best of all ways to find out is to try to assume his outlook and to put yourself in his place. Very well. I may be wrong, but I think, when they're sick of bailing, they'll purchase a pump. And, when that proves useless, as it will, they'll lift up their eyes to the fact that *help they must have*. They won't like the look of that fact, and they'll waste quite a lot of good time trying to find a way round; but at least *they'll accept it*. And that is why it behoves us to drive our tunnel as fast as ever we can."

On the evening of the tenth day, soon after the sun had set, Mansel and Carson and I went out to see what we could. Hanbury had been warned not to return before midnight, for we did not want our reconnaissance to delay or embarrass the relief.

We swam up stream, keeping close to the cliff, each with his clothes and pistol tied up in a wrap of oiled silk and strapped to the back of his head. Soon the cliff gave way to the steep slope of the woods; and at once Mansel, who was leading, took hold of an overhanging bough and swung himself on to dry land and out of sight. Carson and I followed. An immediate observation of the road beyond the river showed that, so far as we could see, there was no one in sight.

We judged that, by going straight up, we should come to the sentinel peak; and, so soon as we had put on our clothes, we began to climb up through the forest in single file.

Either our judgement was at fault, or we bore too much to the left, for, after ten minutes' walking, we saw the walls of the castle a bare thirty paces away. We, therefore, bent to the right and, using extreme caution, made our way under cover to the spot where I had met Bell on the night of the attack on the well.

We were now at the edge of the meadow, and nearly as close to the well as, short of entering the open, a man could come.

The light was fast failing, but as yet we could see well enough.

The redoubt had been finished and now stood some six feet high about the well. I am sure it was loopholed, but this did not appear; probably the loopholes were covered, whilst they were out of use. Of this fastness a third part was roofed, with what I could not distinguish, but rafters had plainly been laid from the wall to the cupola of the well. There was, therefore, some shelter from the heaven; but I could not help thinking that our quarters, grim as they were, were a hundred times more secure and comfortable than this wretched abode, which was, indeed, no better than the byre from which it had sprung.

There was a light burning behind the wall, and once or twice we heard voices; but we could see no movement without, and there was no sound of any labour.

Then Mansel bade Carson and me stay where we were, and himself stole forward along the edge of the wood. He was gone some time, and, when he returned, it was dark. There was, he reported, no sentry that he could locate, nor any sign of the car, which he thought was probably aboard. "If I am right," he added, "there are but three of them here, and to judge from the voices, all those are within the redoubt. We have, therefore, a chance of eavesdropping which may not occur again. And now do exactly as I do; lift up your feet well and mind your step."

With that, he began to step lightly over the grass, making straight for the covered portion of the redoubt; and, a moment later, we were standing beneath its wall, able distinctly to hear every word that was said.

"Live an' let live, Rose," and Punter's voice. "What's the matter with the pump?"

"That," said Rose Noble, "is just what I want to know. If the pump's going to shift the water, why didn't Big Willie have a pump?"

"Cause he didn't have time to go an' get one before we blew in."

"He'd a day and a half," said Rose Noble. "And Big Willie's not the — to dig a hole with his fingers, when he can have a spade."

"A nerror of judgement," said Job. "That's wot it was. They 'ad to choose between goin' an' getting a pump and 'aving a dart with their pails. Directly I see the water, I says, 'Ere's room for a pump.' I know. I 'ad to watch one once."

"Watch one?" said Rose Noble, contemptuously. "What do you mean – 'Watch one'?"

"Watch one," repeated Job. "They 'ave to be watched, of course. But they'll deliver the goods. I tell you, we'll empty this well in a couple of hours. Wait till you see the — a-buzzin' away."

"My God," said Rose Noble, brokenly. "He thinks it's a motor-pump." Punter let out a guffaw. "You — milkmaid, where would we get the power? Where's the current to drive it? Where's the plumbers and masons to set it up? I thought you seemed damned anxious to have a pump. Saw yourself 'watching it,' I suppose – with a bottle of Bass in your pocket and a fag in your face."

"But – "

"It's going to be worked by hand, Job," continued his relentless comforter. "*Your* hand. You will have to work very hard, pushing a bar to and fro. I think it probable that you will sweat. Yes, I thought that'd daze you, you lazy skunk. There's a million down in that well, but, rather than work for a week, you'll let it lie."

"Lazy?" screeched Job. "Lazy? Look at my — hands."

"Oh, I reckon they're dirty," said Rose Noble. "You haven't drawn enough water to rinse them clean." The other's protest he scorched with a terrible oath. "Oh, if I'd 'Holy' Gordon and two of his lads! They didn't care where they slept, whiles the job was raw. They'd 've shifted a — river, if it was keeping gold." He expired violently. "Are you certain sure there's no one in the house?"

"Certain sure," said Punter. "And every mark's as it was. There's no one been through that courtyard for more than a week."

"Then, what's their game?" said Rose Noble, half to himself.

"You can search me," said Punter. "I've dreamed about it o' nights."

"One thing's plain," said the other. "They're banking upon our failure to lick those springs."

125

"An' I don't blame them," muttered Job. "I'd back the —
myself."

Punter disregarded the gloss.

"An', when we've chucked in our hand, they're comin' back."

"That's too easy," said Rose Noble. "Besides, they're a heap
too careful to swallow a risk like that. Big Willie's got his feet up.
But I'd give a bag of money to know his game."

"Rose," said Punter, "they're waitin'. What else can they do?
They didn't half like that bomb. So they gave us the well. But
they're watchin' an' prayin' all right, and, as soon as the pump
starts suckin', they'll show a leg."

"Maybe they will," said Rose Noble. "But don't tell me they're
sitting still. I've seen these Willies before, and they're not that
shape. I'd swear they were digging, but where's their — shaft?"

"Diggin'," said Job. "My Gawd."

"Where's the use?" said Punter. "Say they've drove a tunnel
as far as the well: you'd want half Lancashire to do it, but say
they have. Well, who's going to pull out a brick? There's nothin'
the matter with the treasure, but fifty tons of water waitin' the
other side. Talk about a dam burstin'. You don't have to be an
engineer to – "

"There's a snag somewhere," said Rose Noble. "I can feel it
in my bones. They're moving; I'll swear they're moving; and I
think they're underground. What did they want with the well
that afternoon?"

"They wanted the buckets," said Punter.

"No they didn't," said Rose Noble. "If that was all they were
after, why wouldn't young Willie speak? If you want my opinion,
those buckets are down in the well. When Mansel had got what
he wanted, he just looked around to see what mess he could
make; and the buckets came first."

"You don't say?" said Punter. And then, "The dirty dog."

I was aghast at the man's perspicacity, but Mansel, beside
me, began to shake with laughter.

"The point is," said Rose Noble, "what did Big Willie want?"

No one vouchsafed any answer, and, after a pause, he continued, weighing his words.

"That pup was too blasted glib with his answers about the well. He wasn't lying, but he talked like a guide. Why? I'll give you two answers, and you can take your choice. *Either he was giving us a line which they had found NBG; or else he left out of his budget some one essential fact.*" He hesitated there for a moment. Then he went slowly on, speaking as though to himself. " 'A chamber,' he called it: and then, 'a recess in the wall'."

"That's right," said Punter. "You bet it's a sort of a cell, with a gratin' to keep the bags from washin' away."

"Much more likely walled up," the other replied. "No point in wet gold, if you can have it dry. And there's where I'm bogged," he added violently. "*There's something below they know of that we can't guess.* By — if I knew where they were."

"Might help, might not," said Punter.

" 'Might'?" sneered Rose Noble. " '*Might*'?" I could hear him suck in his breath. "Any one of the six would do; Little Willie, for choice. I shouldn't lose him twice. And I guess he'd see the point of putting us wise. A man mayn't value his life, but he's always devilish sticky about parting with one of his skins."

With his words came the chink of glass, and some liquid was poured.

"Seein's better than believin'," said Punter. "Here's to the — pump."

I suppose that toast was honoured, and, after a moment, somebody rose to his feet.

"You two stay here," said Rose Noble. "I'm going out for a stroll."

Had I been alone, I should have run for cover, and, as like as not, had a bullet in my back for my pains. But Mansel stood fast. By his instant direction, Carson and I lay down while he set his back to the wall, sank his chin on his chest – to hide, as he afterwards told me, the white of his face – and folded his arms.

It seemed an age before Rose Noble passed by, for he went very slowly, as a man in his enemy's camp, and every four or five paces he stood where he was, still as a graven image, using his eyes and ears. Indeed, I shall always believe that the fellow's instinct had told him that we were at hand, for I never saw demeanour so suspicious, and I think that, but for the light of the lamp with which he had just been sitting, which had taken the edge from his vision, he must have perceived Mansel, for he certainly looked straight at him for two or three seconds at a time.

At last, however, the darkness swallowed him up, and Mansel lifted his head. For a moment he stood peering; then he signed to me to lie still and began to steal, like a shadow, the way the other had gone. I was taken aback at his movement, for, armed though he was, to go after the monster alone seemed out of reason. And, when I remembered the humour Rose Noble was in, I broke into a sweat.

It was not Mansel's way to shoot a man in the back, and, since I made sure he was gone to kill Rose Noble, I lay awaiting his challenge with my heart in my mouth. But, after four or five minutes, to my surprise and relief, Mansel emerged from the shadows, as silently as he had gone, and whispered to Carson and me to get to our feet. Then he drew our heads together and spoke in our ears.

"Rose Noble has gone to the castle; while he's out of the way, I'm going to satisfy Punter that we're playing a waiting game. Carson will stay here and watch. If Rose Noble returns, shoot him. If he doesn't, the moment I say 'Good night,' make straight for the sentinel peak. Chandos, you come with me and do as I say."

With that, he walked round the redoubt, with me at his heels. A gap in the wall to the South served as a narrow doorway and suffered the gutter to pass, and, after a careful survey Mansel stepped lightly within.

"Good evening," he said. "Put up your hands, please. And, above all, make no sound."

The prohibition was needless, for Punter and Job were so much dumbfounded that neither of them, I am sure, could have cried out to save his life. Indeed, they sat like two waxworks, staring upon Mansel as though he were an apparition, with their jaws fallen and their eyes bulging out of their heads. Both were unshaven, and Punter was in his socks: a sorry pair of boots was standing on the rim of the well. The covered portion of the fastness was directly opposed to the doorway – above which hung a canvas blind, now hitched to one side – on the farther side of the well; and, since the two were there seated with their backs to the wall, Mansel had stepped to one side to have them in better view.

"Put up your hands," he repeated.

The two obeyed.

Something between them and Mansel stirred in its sleep: and I saw that this was the innkeeper, stretched on the bare ground and tied, like a dog, to one of the pillars of the well. "I'm sorry to intrude," said Mansel, "but I've come all the way from Vichy, and to make such a journey for nothing is not my way. The really annoying thing is I've forgotten my measuring-line; but I dare say you can lend me some cord. William, there's a coil on your left. Just make it fast to that crowbar, and take the depth."

I instantly fell to work, and a moment later the crowbar was descending the well. While I was thus engaged, Mansel continued to talk.

"You see," said he, "though I don't suppose you know it, these springs are intermittent. It's a well-known thing in Natural History, an intermittent spring. It ebbs and flows, you know, rather like the tides of the sea. Well, we have them on the ebb; and, if you'd got down to it that night you'd have had the treasure. I confess I was rather anxious, but when I took the depth the next day, while you were down in the combe, to my intense relief I found that the flood had begun. Now I shouldn't tell you all this if the information would do you the slightest good. But it won't: and I'll tell you why. *Because you don't know when to expect the ebb.* That's where the well-digger's statement is so valuable. Of course you can find out – by the process of – er – exhaustion."

Here I touched bottom and began to pull up the bar.

"When it's up," said Mansel to me, "extend your arms and measure from tip to tip. You're just six feet aren't you?"

I nodded, and he returned to Punter and Job.

"Of course, to get up against Nature is no end of a job. There's a proverb you probably know, which is rather in point. "You can drive Nature out with a pitchfork, *but she'll always come back.*" I know you're not using a pitchfork: you're using a bucket instead. But, pitchfork or bucket, as you see, the result is the same. *She always comes back.*"

The cheerful tone in which Mansel delivered this dismal homily and the unpleasantly obvious pertinence of his remarks had their effect: for Punter looked ready to burst with mortification, and Job was regarding his second comforter with the fishy stare of one who perceives his fortune to be almost too repugnant to be true. Indeed, I had much ado to keep a straight face and I dared not look at Mansel, for, if our eyes had met, I am sure the humour of the case would have been too much for us. I, therefore, busied myself with measuring roughly as much of the cord as was wet, and presently reported my finding of fifty-four feet.

"Dear, dear," said Mansel. "That's shocking. Why, the well will be full before dawn. You might just as well have rested today. Never mind. There's nothing like exercise. And I expect you miss Ellis and Bunch."

That shaft stung Job into speech.

" 'Miss Ellis'?" he groaned. "Oh, good night, nurse!" I was shaking with laughter, but Mansel only smiled.

"I passed them, coming from Salzburg. To be frank I don't think they saw me; but they ought to have known the car. And now I must go. I'm sorry to miss Rose Noble, but you must make my excuses and say I was pressed for time. Good night."

With that he began to go backwards, and I stepped across the redoubt and out of the gap in its wall. The next second Mansel emerged, and we ran like hares for cover towards the sentinel peak.

"Behind a tree," breathed Mansel. "They're certain to fire."

As I whipped round a trunk, somebody fired from the doorway, but the bullet passed over our heads.

"We must wait for Rose Noble," said Mansel. "And while they're putting him wise, we can go on our way. You can't fire straight and argue at one and the same time."

Rose Noble must have been returning, when the shot was fired, for we heard his voice almost at once demanding the truth.

Instead of telling him directly that we were at hand in the wood, both Punter and Job began to report what had passed with an incoherence which would have distracted anyone, and in an instant they were all three raving like men possessed. Under shelter of this exhibition, we beat our retreat, and, presently joining Carson, passed over the shoulder of the hill and back the way we had come.

We were well pleased with what we had found, but the head and front of our contentment was naturally furnished by Mansel's brilliant stroke. Indeed, I cannot believe that the shrewdest of diplomats ever delivered a more dexterous thrust: and, when it is remembered that Mansel's performance was improvised, that he conceived and executed it with his life, so to speak, in his hand, I think it will be clear that he was a man of lightning apprehension and notable detachment.

By his admirable fable of the intermittent springs he had offered an answer, at once most credible and gloomy, to every one of the problems that troubled the thieves, and had hanged a very mill-stone about Rose Noble's neck, for, by confirming the bulk of the suspicions which the latter had openly avowed, he had highly prejudiced such efforts to hearten his fellows as the monster might presently make.

Indeed, as we afterwards learned, for a fortnight after his exploit, next to no water was taken out of the well, but Rose Noble spent all of his time quelling mutinies, eating his own words and striving by hook or by crook to hold the gang together against some future attempt. That in this he succeeded does him, to my mind, great credit, for I have shown many times how ill he was served and what poor stomachs for work or for danger the other thieves had.

And here let me say that, to give the devil his due, Rose Noble possessed a commanding personality, swift, vigilant and unearthly strong; and, behind it, like some familiar, stood his astounding instinct, continually showing him things which no manner of wisdom or prudence could ever have perceived. It seems he never ceased to maintain that we were digging, and that with a conviction so infectious, although he could not produce one jot or title of warrant for what he said, the others came to accept this surmise as an established fact, and, though they would draw no water, to search with more or less diligence for any sign of a shaft. And that was, I think, a remarkable achievement: and, as is sometimes the way, it had its reward.

No one of us will ever forget the ninth night of June.

That day we had driven our shaft as far as the point from which Mansel had taken the bearing of the well, that is to say, we had covered just eighty-one yards; and there we had altered our course so as to head directly for where the chamber must lie. It seemed certain that eighty-nine yards, at the most, remained to be pierced; but we had fair reason to think that the distance would prove to be less, and that, when we had covered another eighty yards, we might expect any moment to strike the chamber. We were, therefore, come roughly half-way to the region we sought; and this elated us all, as did the knowledge that the thieves were making no serious endeavour to empty the well; for, though because of their vigilance we had been unable again to approach the redoubt, we had twice visited the spot upon which the gutter discharged and found it comparatively dry.

It was Hanbury's turn to relieve Mansel; the night was warm and moonlit, and there was no wind at all.

The relief was more than half done; Carson, indeed, had already descended the shoot, and Mansel was stripped to the waist, *when we heard Tester give tongue.*

Sharp and clear, across the water came his deep, vigorous bark, bold and menacing.

For an instant we stood breathless, staring at the three long windows, through which the sound had come. Then, in a flash, Mansel had entered the shoot. I followed immediately, clad only in a zephyr and shorts, and was in the boat almost as soon as he. Without a word Carson bent to the sculls, and the craft leaped forward.

Our passage, usually so soon over, seemed that night as though it would never be done, and I well remember remarking how lovely the landscape looked, and what a queer contrast we offered – all of us dripping, and Carson, except for his shoes, mother-naked. All the time Tester was baying someone furiously.

We were unarmed, and, as we came to the bank:

"Single file, please," said Mansel. "We mustn't bunch. And, when we come to the track, you will bear to the right and Carson to the left."

I had the painter, and, before I had made fast the boat, Mansel and Carson were ashore and out of my sight.

Now the track which led to the quarry lay seventy paces or so from the river's bank, some half of which they had run before I was out of the boat. An impression was, therefore, given that we were but two, and I ran straight into some stranger at the mouth of the track. He had clearly let the others go and was making good his escape. He was a giant of a man, but I am no feather-weight, and the shock of our encounter sent us both to the ground. I was up in an instant, but he was quicker, and, what was worse, fleeter of foot, for although I pursued him West for a mile or more, he gradually drew away and I had to give up his pursuit.

I then returned to the quarry, to Mansel's evident relief; for all he had heard was our fall, and, before he had been able to reach the mouth of the track, the stranger and I were out of earshot. The car did not seem to have been touched, and no one of her locks had been tampered with; Tester was safe and sound; neither Mansel nor Carson had seen or heard anyone, and it seemed likely that the man I had chased had been the sole occasion of Tester's wrath. Particularly to describe him, however, was beyond my power, for we had met in the shadows and I had not seen his face. He was not one of the thieves nor yet the innkeeper; and, unless they had been reinforced, there was little to suggest that he had to do with the enemy, or, indeed, was anything more to be feared than an inquisitive peasant who had noticed George Hanbury's arrival and found his behaviour strange. As such we found him unwelcome, but, if he was to see us no more, harmless. Yet, there was about the business one curious, disquieting fact, slight in its way as any ghost, yet one that we could not lay.

The fellow was a tanner by trade. That I could swear, for he reeked of the tannery. Now, I have always found an odour more reminiscent than even a melody, and I have but to become

aware of some perfume to remember directly the circumstances in which I have smelt it before. Yet, though, the
moment I scented the fellow, I knew I had encountered his like
or his occupation quite recently, for the life of me I could not
recall when or where it had been, and no artifice of Mansel's
could bring it back to my mind, but we could not help feeling
that, if here was a clue to the interloper's identity, it would be
highly imprudent to cast it away; and, for myself, I was puzzled,
for it was unlike my memory, having got so far, to be able to get
no further. At last, however, we set aside the riddle, for there
was work to be done, and, as Mansel said with reason,
"sometimes the brain is mulish, and will do better if you put up
your cudgel and let it be."

Our policy had been always to take no avoidable risk, and,
since the car had been discovered, our store of timber also had
been remarked, we at once decided to get as much of this as
the cover of night would allow into the *oubliette*. As a rule, the
relief had brought enough wood to last us for twenty-four hours,
and this much had been delivered by Hanbury and Rowley that
night; but, since without timber to advance the shaft would be
at least a very perilous business, to transfer every balk that we
could seemed but a natural precaution.

We, therefore, set about this removal without more ado.
Rowley was brought to help us, while Hanbury and Bell stayed
to receive the wood. We laboured with all our might till an hour
before dawn, by which time we had carried a great deal, though
not, it appeared, so much as we had already employed.

We made no attempt to find a fresh hiding-place for the car;
for, for one thing, we had no mind to leave her any more
unattended, and, for another, it seemed better in future to berth
her each night at a different point, so that, if our visit was
expected, at least we should not be playing clean into some
peeper's hands. The boat and sculls we decided to bestow in a
culvert some four miles away, for they were nothing to carry,

and, to take them up, as we passed, would be but a moment's work.

The sky was pale when Rowley and I stood again in the gallery, and before Mansel could come to Salzburg, we knew that the sun would be high; but the smell of the timber all about us did our hearts good, and we lay down to sleep for an hour in the comfortable state of a garrison whose store of munitions is no longer without the fort.

Now, whether it was this reflection or the scent of the sawn wood that jogged my memory I cannot tell; but my mind whipped back to the tanner, and in a twinkling I remembered when and where I had noticed his particular odour before. And that put an end to my slumber before it was ever begun, and to that of the others as well; for, though I had clean forgotten it, I now recalled perfectly that *I had become aware of the smell of tan at one and the same instant that I was felled from behind on that night of alarms and excursions when Mansel was down in the well.*

7

Rose Noble Moves

There was, naturally, much to be said; but, till Mansel returned to the dungeon, there was nothing to be done. And, since the commentary he made, so soon as he heard my news, was far more valuable than the swarm of conclusions which we had drawn out of the matter, I will set it down, using his words.

"A great deal is depending on how much the tanner saw. If he saw two come in the car, the presence of a third must have told him that we have some hiding-place hereabouts; if he saw the relief carrying timber, that should make him think; but, if he saw the boat cross the river, he must know a damned sight too much. And it was a moonlit night.

"The point is – what will he do?

"His instinct will be to put the innkeeper wise. But the innkeeper is in balk. He will, therefore, endeavour to communicate with him without the knowledge of the thieves. And the only way to do that is through the inn.

"Now, I think it more likely that now and again the landlord returns to his inn – *under escort*, of course. Otherwise, long before now, a hue and cry would have been raised. And that wouldn't suit Rose Noble. About once a week, I imagine, they take him back to the inn; and they give him to understand that, if he gets out of the car, that's the last living movement he'll

137

make. Again, he has, without doubt, been straitly advised that upon the first sign of any attempt at his rescue he will immediately die. If they've got these things into his head – and, though he can't speak German, from what I've seen of Rose Noble, I should say he was above Babel – not fifty home-sweet-homes will drag him out of that car; and he probably tells his people that he's having the time of his life. And that's the way, I expect, they get their supplies.

"Very well. If the tanner tells the innkeeper, what will the latter do? *I think it more than likely that he will give us away.* I don't say he'll do so deliberately; but the tanner's tidings will startle him, and, unless he's alone to receive them – and that is most improbable – the thieves will perceive his emotion and demand to be told its cause.

"The first thing to do, therefore, is to visit the inn. If I had known this last night, I'd have gone there today. As it is, we must wait. I imagine that trouble is coming; but, unless the luck is against us, I don't think it's coming just yet."

And that, for the moment, was as much as Mansel said; but, as later that night I sailed through the sleeping country towards St Martin, I could not help wondering whether I was not making this now familiar journey for the last time, and, though the next day was fair as a day can be, I had no pleasure in it, and the pastime of fishing seemed to have lost its savour. Yet, I might have spared my concern; for, when I returned to the dungeon, it was to find all well, and throughout the relief we seemed to have the world to ourselves.

That night Mansel and Hanbury visited the track below the combe, but found no sign of water drawn out of the well. When Bell and I were come, we began to take in more wood; by dint of working till cock-crow without a break, we carried all that was left, to our comfort more of mind than of body, for, when it was all under ground, we could hardly move.

While we were thus engaged, some fifteen yards of our tunnel started to bulge and had to be shored up before we continued the shaft.

The next day Mansel visited Lerai and ate his lunch at the inn. The landlord's wife proved only too willing to talk, and the first thing that Mansel learned was that her husband seemed to have thrown in his lot with the thieves, though what in the world they were doing and where they were she could not tell. With that, she had wrung her hands and presently thrown her apron over her head, declaring with tears that, if there were rogue's company to be had, her lord would be sure to find it, though it lay a day's journey off; for his mother had been a Roman, and, though she had died at his birth, the blood of lawlessness was in his veins. Then Mansel drew a bow at a venture and, observing that he would have thought that rogues in Carinthia were few, casually spoke of a tanner as the one rustic we had met that had worn the look of a knave. At once the hostess had let out a gush of abuse, avowing that the man and his brother were the black sheep of that part of the land, that her husband knew them well, and had harboured one for a fortnight when a warrant was out for his arrest. *On the last two days*, she added, *the tanner had come to the inn, and, despite her insistence that her husband was away on a journey, had each time stayed for some hours, as though in a hope of his return. But on neither of those two days had the closed car come, as it did from time to time, to take up all manner of food.* And here she fell to raving about the stranger's score, by now amounting to some seventy English pounds, of which not one penny had been paid, declaring that here was the proof that her husband's union with the thieves was something sinister, for that he was strict as a bailiff where debts were concerned. "However," says she in the end, "no wind's so ill that it blows no scruple of good, for the strangers' ways may be evil, but the tanner's are worse; and, at last, my husband is out of some villainy, for, now that the tanner has twice gone empty away, I do not think he will return."

Herein we hoped very much that the woman was right; for, if the tanner's discovery came to the knowledge of the thieves, our valuable system of reliefs would certainly be imperilled, if not destroyed, to say nothing of the fact that they would instantly know that we were driving a shaft.

I have shown already that, since our brush with the tanner, we berthed the car each night at some different place; but Mansel was not satisfied with this precaution, and presently determined that the relief should always begin at eleven o'clock, and that, from ten o'clock onward, one of the four in the dungeon should watch as much as he could of the opposite shore. This may appear to have been an idle exercise, because the sentry was too distant to see or hear any movement which was made in the danger zone; and I must confess that I did not myself account it worth the expense of a workman – for nowadays we laboured to all hours; but Mansel had given the order, and so it was done.

We had always kept in the dungeon a supply of tinned food, sufficient to last us some days: but this stock we now increased, until, if the worst came to pass, we could live for full three weeks without leaving the *oubliette*.

However, the day went by and no one troubled us; if the tanner watched us again, we never saw him; the soil at the foot of the gutter was sometimes drenched, but never the marsh we had made it; and, while the enemy's labour was fitful, and they had, I think, no concerted plan of action, except to deny us the well, we continued to drive forward with all our might.

And here let me say that we were by now the owners of Wagensburg; for Ellis had let go his option, and Mansel had purchased the place. But I doubt if seigniory was ever so strangely enjoyed – the freeholders having their being, like rats, in the bowels of the earth, and in constant dread of their presence being observed, and their enemies in possession and coming and going and doing just as they pleased.

It was thirteen days to an hour since Tester had bayed the tanner, and Bell and I were engaged at the nose of the shaft, when I heard someone running towards us, and, in the next moment, Rowley's voice. Hanbury desired me, he said, to come to the gallery at once.

Leaving Bell to put out the searchlight and follow me down, I immediately left for the gallery, making what haste I could; but, after the glare of the lamp, I was as good as blind, and the light of the candles which were burning in the shaft and the *oubliette*, was too feeble to guide my steps.

However, at last I was down, to find Hanbury at the middle embrasure, peering into the night.

His report was disquieting indeed.

"There's someone across the river: I saw the flash of a torch."

I do not think either of us doubted that the fat was now in the fire, for that anyone but one of the thieves would be using an electric torch about the quarry, or, indeed, for twenty miles round, was most improbable.

The time was half past ten; and Mansel was due to arrive at eleven o'clock.

Now where he would berth that Rolls we could not tell, beyond that it would be at some place within five hundred yards of the spot we had used as a quay; but, since there were but two roads – the one running South from Villach and into the other, which followed the river along – for the thieves to mark her arrival would be most easy; and, once they had seen her stop and her occupants separate, the most maladroit attack could hardly fail.

There was, therefore, but one thing to do, namely, to try to reach Mansel before the Rolls had entered the danger zone; and, since he was always punctual, yet never hurried, it was perfectly plain that, if we were to be in time, we had not one moment to lose.

In a twinkling, our plans were laid.

Hanbury, who was a good runner, was to make the attempt; having swum the river and landed a little down stream, he was to strike across country and head for the Villach road. Bell and I were to follow, but, when we had crossed the river, we should approach the quarry and try to locate the thieves, so that, if Hanbury failed, at least we should be able to offer some other support. Rowley was to be left in charge of the *oubliette*.

Hanbury was gone in an instant, for he was lightly clad and waited for nothing; but for Bell and me to go unarmed would have been idle, and, since we must wrap up our pistols to save them from getting wet, we stripped and did the same with our clothes, before descending the shoot.

We were soon across the water, and, having made the bank at a place where a gurgling brook ran into the river, were able to dress in its gully without much apprehension of being heard.

Indeed, the night itself was an invisible cloak; I never remember darkness so impenetrable; and there was not a breath of air.

I then did my best to consider what manner of ambush the thieves would determine to lay, but could only decide that the track which led to the quarry and the junction of the two roads were, for the moment, the two most probable points; we, therefore, crossed the road and began to move towards the junction, in the hope of hearing some sound which would help us to a better understanding of what was afoot. The track which led to the quarry ran out of the Villach road.

We had come, so far as I could judge, to within fifteen yards of the junction, when I heard the murmur of a voice a little way off. I at once stood still, the better to hear whence it came, but even as I did so, it ceased. After straining my ears in vain, I went cautiously on, to be instantly checked by a rope, stretched breast high across the road, and stout enough to stop or disable a car that sought to pass by. This discovery shook me, for it showed that the thieves not only knew what to expect, but intended to take no chance of losing their prey. However, I was thankful to have made it; and, since Bell had with him his knife, we immediately severed the rope and let it lie.

It now seemed certain that, if we went on, past the junction we should come to another rope, for to bar but one of two doors would have been out of reason; it was also equally clear that we had now come to the verge of the danger zone, and that this lay, roughly triangular, about the junction, with its base running directly from rope to rope, and its apex lying somewhere upon the Villach road.

Since I had no plan of action, to open the road, if we could, seemed plainly the first thing to do; and, with this intent, we picked our way to the river and started to hug its edge, in order to give the junction as wide a berth as we could.

We had reached a point opposite the junction, and, from where I was standing, I could see the pale smear which the Villach road made upon the black of the night, when I felt Bell's fingers close upon my arm. I suppose his grip was tell-tale, for, though he breathed no word, in that instant I certainly knew that the worst had happened, and that *Hanbury had lost his race.*

So we stood, still as death, for five seconds; then I heard the brush of a tyre, as it rounded a hairpin bend.

I have heard it said that, though the approach of a crisis is apt to scatter the wits, its sudden descent will sometimes whip them back into a battle array. So it was with me at that moment, for, though for a quarter of an hour I had been groping feverishly, my disorder suddenly left me, and I saw as clear as daylight what I must do.

At once I drew my pistol and fired twice across the road.

I thought the consequent din would never die; but at last the echoes faded, and we were able to listen for lesser sounds.

The Rolls had stopped.

Now, though we had ruined the ambush, there was still the devil to pay, for I knew the way was too narrow to let the Rolls go about, and that to reverse in such darkness along so crooked a road was out of the question. But it suddenly came to my mind that if Mansel were to switch on his headlights and run for it towards Lerai, that is to say *turn to the left at the junction*, we should be out of the wood; for the thieves would almost certainly suffer the car to go by in the full expectation that she would be wrecked by the rope. I, therefore, decided to join Mansel as quickly as ever I could and, whispering to Bell to follow, hastened across the foreshore and on to the road.

Pitch-dark though it was, I dared not go directly by way of the Villach road, and we had just started back towards Lerai, when I heard the deep breath of an engine, and then the Rolls coming, with the rush of a mighty wind.

Mansel had divined the best course, and was making his dash. And all would be well, *provided he turned to the left*. If, *at the junction, he turned to the right instead...*

I know that for one long moment my heart stood still.

Then, throwing caution to the winds, Bell and I turned and raced for the second rope.

The junction was now bright as day, and the car was so close that, had there been nothing to gain, I should not have crossed its path, but have waited for it to go by. I found myself praying that Mansel would turn to the left. As he swooped at the corner I ran clean into the rope, but the Rolls was round and *coming* before I had opened Bell's knife. I slashed at the rope like a madman, but before I could cut it right through the car swept by, and, ripping it out of my hand, mercifully snapped asunder such strands as were left.

As we ran in the wake of the Rolls, I heard an ejaculation and then a spurt of high words, but, though I was sure I heard Ellis, I could not distinguish Rose Noble's voice.

The Rolls had vanished, and I was beginning to wonder whether it would not be wiser to let Bell go on, while I returned to see what the thieves were doing and, if I could, meet Hanbury, when Mansel rose out of the shadows and spoke my name.

I told him my tale.

"I'm much obliged," he said quietly. "You were up against time and the thieves, and you beat them both. When I am so placed, I hope I shall do as well. I think it likely that Hanbury missed his way; it's very hard to go straight on a night like this. And that's why we must get back. Your shots will bring him to the junction, and we don't want an accident."

With that, he showed us the boat and the sculls in a ditch, and proposed to take to the water and scull down stream.

"For the way of a river," said he, "is swift and safe and silent, and I was a fool not to have used it before."

In this he was unfair to himself, for the relief nowadays took up the best part of an hour, four water journeys having to be made each night, and, if these journeys had been considerably lengthened, we should have been worn out before we could get to bed.

Then he told us that the Rolls was gone, and would not come back that way; but that Carson had orders to be at the culvert at three, and, if no one of us came before four o'clock, to return to Salzburg. Before he went, he would leave a note wedged in the brickwork, to say he was safe, and when twenty-four hours had gone by, he would come there again. So he would continue to do, until one of us came to meet him or he found a note under the arch.

"And now for Hanbury," said Mansel: "and then for the *oubliette*."

We slipped down the river noiselessly, and, when we approached the bend, at a signal from Mansel, Bell, who was rowing, rested upon his oars. We could hear no sound at all, and, after drifting for a moment, Mansel whispered to Bell to head for the shoot.

So thick was the darkness that Bell, not unnaturally, sculled to the side of the stream and, when he could make out the bank, began to follow this down.

We had just passed the slope of the woods and come to the cliff, when a torch was flashed twice from the bank five paces away. Before we could think, came two flashes from the opposite side.

And that was all.

At once Bell lay on his oars; but, after listening intently, Mansel bade him scull for the shoot.

Almost at once we were there, and Mansel put up a hand and rang the bell.

So soon as the flap was lifted: "Listen, Rowley," says Mansel, putting his mouth to the shoot. "Is Mr Hanbury with you?"

"No, sir."

"Have you anything to report?"

"Two flashes a moment ago, sir; but nothing else."

Mansel turned to me.

"William," he said, "I don't think we're out of the wood. To be perfectly honest, I'm altogether at sea. I know neither what to do nor what to think. But what bothers me most of all is – *where is Rose Noble?* That being so, I'd rather you held the fort. So you go up, and send Rowley down to me. And then we'll go and find George."

I did not at all relish the prospect of garrison duty at such a time; for, if trouble was coming, to be mewed up within sound of the skirmish would be well-nigh unbearable. But, since I had nothing to plead but my own reluctance, I stripped with what haste I could, and, two minutes later, Rowley had taken my place.

The night was so dark and so still that, for a moment, I thought the windows were shuttered, and was stupidly astonished to find the timbers gone; and, when I looked out, I might have been gazing into a bottomless pit. However, I took my seat in the middle embrasure and, cupping my chin in my palm, stared resolutely into the darkness, with my ears pricked to gather the faintest sound. But all I could hear was the regular lap of the water against the face of the cliff.

It had all along been in my mind that Mansel and Hanbury would cross; and, when, but a short five minutes after the former had left, the bell from the shoot announced the latter's return, I was less surprised than provoked by this well-worn trick of fortune; for there was Mansel gone out on a sleeveless errand into the midst of some danger he could not read, and that at a time when the last thing we needed to do was to play the spy and everything was to be gained by lying close below ground.

However, the milk was spilt; and, since to tread water is a laborious exercise, I lost no time in setting aside the flap and letting the ladder down.

It was immediately clear that George was very near spent, for, when I called to him he had not the breath to answer and when at last he was fairly upon the ladder, he hung there, panting, like a dog on a sultry day. I asked if I should come down, but he took no notice, and, after a little while, he began to ascend. I was alarmed by his demeanour, which was that of the survivor of some catastrophe, and, squatting down at the head of the ladder, reached out my hands to help him out of the shoot.

Now, I had intended to set my hands under his arms, but the moment I touched him he threw an arm round my neck. To save myself from falling I instinctively flung myself back and, since in that instant he heaved, the two of us fell down together on to the flags.

"Thanks very much," said Rose Noble.

Then I felt the mouth of a pistol pressed tight against my throat.

I can never describe the disgust and the horror I felt; but the brain is a curious member, and, as I lay there on the pavement, with the bulk of his body upon me, I could not help thinking that Rose Noble's ascent of the shoot was a remarkable feat for a man of his corpulent habit, and wondering how he had made it without the support of an oath.

He was lightly clad, but the clothes he was wearing were drenched; and the absurd conceit that I was in the clutches of some aquatic monster was most repugnant. Nevertheless, I had the sense to lie still; and, after a little, Rose Noble got to his knees.

For a moment he fumbled; then the bright eye of a torch illumined the chamber.

At this my heart leaped up, for had he desired to appraise Mansel of his entry, he could not have found a surer or swifter way; for all three windows were open, and their sudden radiance was bound to publish my plight.

Rose Noble got to his feet and bade me do the same. I was glad to obey. Then he stepped back and looked about him.

"So," he said, after a while. Then he leaned forward and spoke down the shoot. "Bunch."

"Hullo," said Bunch from below.

"You saw me ring that bell?"

"Yes," said Bunch.

"Fetch Ellis and Job over here. When you're back, ring three times."

"Right-o."

Rose Noble straightened his back.

"Pull up that ladder," he said.

"Not on your life," said I. "You've come to the wrong house."

I could hardly see him, for the light was full in my face, but I felt his eyes upon mine.

At length he took a deep breath.

Then: "Stand back," he said, thickly.

I did so, folding my arms.

At once he straddled the shoot, and, putting the torch in his teeth, with his free hand felt for the ladder and pulled it up. Then he picked up the flap and sank this into its place.

This show of strength surprised me, for the flap was very heavy, and I would never have believed that a man so fat and flabby could have made light of such a task.

Rose Noble took the torch from his mouth and leaned his
back against the wall.

"When Ellis comes," said he, "I shall ask you to show us
around. I like to think that you will grant that request." I said
nothing, and after a moment he continued slowly enough.
"Nobody likes getting stuck; but, when he's stuck good and
proper, the wise guy swallows his dose. And now, listen to me,
you young fool. I've taken possession here, *and here I stay*, so
long as I stay, Mansel will remain outside; he's very welcome to
get up that drain – if he can; but, short of the ladder, I don't
believe he'll try. If he wants the well, he can have it, but I rather
fancy he'll be thinking more about you – they say blood's
thicker than water... Well, he's welcome to think. If he asks me,
I haven't seen you; I found the ladder waiting and came right up."

"D'you think he'll believe you?" said I.

"Why not?" said Rose Noble.

I had no answer to make, for, as I spoke, I saw the force of
his words. Here truth was stranger than fiction; and Mansel
would never believe that I had handed him in.

"And so," said Rose Noble quietly, "I guess we can count
Mansel out."

"Don't you believe it," said I. "He's made rings round you in
the past, and he'll do it again."

"Maybe he will," said Rose Noble. "But unless and until he
does, I reckon *it's up to you.*"

"Indubitably," said I.

Rose Noble sighed.

"No fool like a young fool," he said. Then he leaned forward.
"Why put me up, when you haven't a card in your hand?"

I shrugged my shoulders.

"Much cry, but little wool," said I. "Come to the point. Are
you trying to do a deal?"

"Yes," said Rose Noble. "I am. Maybe it's a shade one-sided;
but you gave it that name." He jerked his torch at the ramp
which led to the *oubliette*. "I've yet to see these diggings; but I

haven't played 'King o' the Castle' for a whole raft of years, and I guess it'll save us all time if you give me the book of the rules. In return, I offer you a painless captivity, a hell of a lot of hard work, and a free pass-out three days after we touch."

I laughed.

"It is one-sided," said I, as cheerfully as I could.

"These sort of deals often are," was the grim reply.

I could not think what to do.

I was unarmed, for I had left my pistol for Rowley when he had taken my place; the other fire-arms hung upon a wall of the chamber, all of them loaded, but all of them out of my reach. Yet, had they lain by my side, the fellow had me in check; and I knew that, were I to move, he would shoot me down. For all that, my case was nothing to what it must be when Ellis and Job were come. Till then, at least, we were but man to man; but, if Rose Noble was able to bring but one of them up, I was as good as lost; and so was our enterprise. That I must, therefore, take action before they could enter the shoot was very evident, and I saw at once that when he went to admit them was the moment to make my attempt. His torch, of course, was his blessing and my unspeakable curse; but for this we should have been better matched, for, though he had his pistol, I knew my way about and was, indeed, accustomed to moving in the gallery without any light. I, therefore, determined, somewhat desperately, that, when he stooped for the flap, by hook or by crook I must dash the torch from his mouth, and, if I could not there and then follow up this assault, at least to jump to one side and so out of his ken.

And here it came to me that, so far as his torch was concerned, my luck was indeed dead out; for if ever any one of us went up or down the shoot without saving his torch from the water, whether because he forgot it or took the chance, so surely that torch was useless and would give no glimmer of light until it had been looked to and its battery changed.

So we stood, with the flap between us, I trying to watch Rose Noble behind the glare of the torch, he with his eyes upon mine, and both of us, I fancy, awaiting the throb of the bell.

At length: "Well," said Rose Noble.

I moistened my lips.

"There's nothing doing," said I. "Of course, you can do me in, but it won't help you. For one thing, I'm not going to talk; for another, I've nothing to say, for – believe me or not, as you please – it's Mansel and Hanbury together that do the sums. You talk about guys that get stuck, why, you've never been anything else. You've been stuck at the top of the well – "

"See here," said Rose Noble thickly, "when I want a — lecture, I'll let you know. Meantime I'll give you a hunch, and that is, *get right with God.*" The man's hand was shaking; and I think this angered him, for he let out a frightful oath. "You say you're not going to talk," he continued presently. "Well, *there's your right eye gone.* I don't set up for a surgeon, but my hand don't always shake, and an inch of red-hot wire makes a nice, clean job. And, maybe, when you're short of a light, you'll find your tongue; it's not an operation you'll find in the medical books, but by God, *I've known it work.*"

I suppose that the monster saw that his words had shocked me – as, indeed, to be honest, they had; for, while they were dreadful enough, the meaning with which he spoke them was unmistakable; at any rate he laughed hideously – the fat laugh of a satyr, that made my blood run cold.

And, as he laughed, the light of his torch went out. We were both of us taken by surprise; but for this particular accident he, I imagine, was more unready than I, and, though he fired, he was an instant too late, for I had taken my chance and leaped to the right.

The crash of the explosion covered what noise I made, and, before the racket was over, I was at the foot of the ramp, straining my ears.

I heard him grope for my body and curse when he found me gone. The next moment he fired again, and the bullet parted my hair. He must have fired at a venture; but so good was the shot that it seemed as though he could see, and I turned and fled up the ramp, like a startled hare.

Now, before I had taken ten steps, I saw the faint glow of the candles alight in the *oubliette*; these I had clean forgotten, but now in a flash I knew that I could not have made a more unfortunate move, for, having escaped from one light, here I was making my way towards another. To make matters worse, as I perceived my mistake, I missed my footing and fell, making the deuce of a noise, and in an instant I heard Rose Noble behind.

There was now nothing for it but to go on up the ramp, for this was far too narrow for me to let him go by; indeed, I fully expected that he would fire again, but I suppose he was minded to husband his shots. I, therefore, went rapidly on and had just decided to make a dash for the candles and put them out, if I could, before Rose Noble could reach the *oubliette*, when he let out a "Ha" of triumph, which showed me that he had viewed the glimmer ahead.

Now the slightest reflection would have told me that, moving from him to the glow, which was actually framed by the postern at the head of the ramp, I was offering such a target as no marksman could very well miss; and I think he must surely have been upon the edge of bringing me down, when the bell from the shoot was rung. Perhaps he held his hand to hear if it rang again, but, if so, he lost his chance, for I suddenly perceived my folly and fell on my face. As I did so, the bell rang again; and then a third time.

At once Rose Noble began to descend the ramp.

There was but one thing to do, and that was to follow him down. Once Ellis and Job were in, my race was as good as run. So down I went, moving beneath the shelter of the noise that he made – for till you had the way of it the descent of the ramp was a difficult exercise – and racking my brain for some fair opportunity of giving battle.

The rifles and, certainly, two pistols were hanging upon the West wall, that is to say, about three feet from the shoot; we kept them there on purpose that they might be always convenient to anyone leaving the chamber; but, for me, they could not have hung in a more unfortunate place, and I could not think how to reach them without Rose Noble's knowledge that I was at hand.

Suddenly my heart leaped, and I thought of the wood.

At the eastern end of the gallery lay some timber, for we had not carried it all into the *oubliette*; and, though a joist was plainly a clumsy weapon to ply within four walls, I was cheered by the thought that it was also a formidable arm and possessed the clear advantage of a considerable range.

I, therefore, made haste to come down to the foot of the ramp, but, as I gained the chamber, I heard Rose Noble setting aside the flap. How he had been so quick I cannot tell, but I saw in an instant that, if I was to dispute the entrance of Ellis and Job, I had not a second to lose. As I groped for the timber, I heard the ladder go down, and at that moment I touched a case of tinned food. This was open. Without waiting to think, I picked up a tin – what it contained I know not; but I think it was fruit – and hurled it with all my might at where Rose Noble must be. I know that it hit him, for he let out a cry of pain, but, before he could fire, I had flung another tin.

The case was full, and I had discharged five tins before I heard him coming with a volley of oaths. Instantly I whipped to the ramp and, as he went by, darted to the opposite wall. In a moment I had a pistol and, as he fired into the timber, I jerked up the ladder and, thrusting my arm into the shoot itself, fired directly into the water below. That this would discourage Ellis I felt very sure; and, since he had no instructions except to ring the bell, he could hardly be blamed, if, after such a reception, he beat a retreat. But there was still Rose Noble; and I knew very well that, though I had prevented his fellows, I had done so at the price of provoking most deeply the wrath of this terrible man. And, indeed, in a moment I heard a sound which told me that what had gone by was a skirmish and that the battle à *outrance* was just about to begin. I heard the long, heavy breathing of a man who is out to kill.

I had never heard it before, but it is a sound as fearful as it is expressive; and I must honestly confess that, when I heard it, I was frightened to death. However, I tried to take heart by thinking that the odds were in my favour, for now we both were armed and I was not only the more agile, but knew our surroundings as the palm of my hand.

My first impulse was to fire in that direction from which the breathing came; but then I saw that the flash of my pistol would betray me and that, unless I hit him, before I could move, he would return my shot. And there, of course, he had the advantage of me, for, while I knew little of fire-arms, beyond that they must be handled with infinite care, Rose Noble gave the impression of being as ready with a pistol as are most men with a pen. Yet, strange as it seems, I found his bullets far less dreadful than his presence itself, and the thought that he must be approaching pricked me to make a move.

The first thing I did was to stumble upon the flap, and at once I heard him move forward towards the shoot. Instinctively, I shrank back, to find myself in the corner of the North and West walls. How I had missed the shoot I do not know, but there it was at my feet; I could feel its current of air.

If I did not move now, I was lost – that is to say unless I could kill my man; for I was literally cornered, and, if Rose Noble came on, he would, any moment now, cut off my escape. I, therefore, stole to my left and had come to the first embrasure, some five feet away, when something swept past my chin and, then, lightly touching the wall on my left, sailed horizontally back, missing me this time by a hair's breadth.

Again I recoiled, thus making my second mistake, for an instant later I knew he had picked up a helve and with this was sweeping the chamber to find me out. The moment the helve had sailed back I should have advanced; but I had let the chance go.

I was now fairly back in my corner, when again I heard the helve touch – this time the wall on my right. This to my horror, for it showed that the cast which Rose Noble was making was almost done and that in four or five seconds the fellow's terrible instinct would have its reward.

I, therefore, dropped on one knee and set my left hand on the flags, the better to steady my aim; but I knew that the odds were against me, because the moment he touched me he would know where to fire, whilst I could not possibly tell to within some two or three feet.

Rose Noble moved like a cat, giving no sound. Only the helve touched again, this time very close. I could hear the lap of the water and feel the air from the shoot flirting my face. And then, all of a sudden, I saw a bare chance of escape.

The flap, when sunk into place, lay flush with the pavement, and so supported by a ledge running around the shoot, cut out of the stone. This ledge was two inches in width – wide enough to give handhold to a desperate man.

Hardly waiting to pocket my pistol, I entered the shoot, and a moment later I was altogether out of the gallery, yet able to re-enter at will, hanging by my hands from the ledge, staring up into the chamber to mark what I could.

I heard Rose Noble above me, tapping all around with the helve; I could hear his breathing quite close, and something wet fell from him on to my upturned face. This was blood, so I knew that I must have cut him with one of the tins. Suddenly I heard him stiffen and hold his breath. Then he turned round; and, as in a theatre, by some trick of production to pretend the coming of dawn, you may see the forms of men grow gradually out of the darkness, *so I saw the monster begin to take shape.*

He was standing crouched, with his knees well bent and his left leg a little advanced; his great head was up and his jaw jutted out like a peak; in his left hand he held the helve and in his right was his pistol, pointed and ready to fire; his pistol arm was crooked and steady as a rock.

He had but to drop his eyes for them to light upon me; but he did not, keeping them fixed, instead, upon what I judged must be the foot of the ramp.

All this I saw at first dimly, but gradually more and more clearly, to my great astonishment; for the effect was magical, and I could think of no earthly explanation.

Then in a flash my brain cleared, and I knew it for the work of the searchlight, which Mansel or Hanbury was carrying down the ramp. They must have entered the dungeon by way of the trap and, hearing no sound from the gallery, were hastening thither in a concern for me which could wait upon no risks.

And here was I out of action; and there was Rose Noble, like a fowler, watching a bird come down into his snare.

There was only one thing to be done.

"Look out! It's Rose Noble!" I yelled, and let myself go.

It was a rough passage and cost me a lot of skin; but, of course, I fell down like a stone and was, I suppose, under water before Rose Noble had recovered from his surprise. For he never fired.

A moment later I was swimming down stream.

And that was the end of my adventure; for I had hardly landed upon the castle side, when out of the forest came Rowley and asked me if I was unhurt.

At first I thought I was dreaming, but he said that he had come straight from the staircase-turret, after letting the others into the *oubliette*. His orders were to put back the slabs, destroy every trace of their removal and then lie close in the woods till break of day. He was then to cross the river, and, if he saw a towel in a window, to come to the shoot.

But I would not wait so long, because I feared that, finding me gone, when he had dispatched Rose Noble, Mansel would go out in my quest. So, since the boat was at hand, we at once sculled back to the shoot and there, sure enough, met Mansel about to go out after Rowley and then after me.

"Are you hurt?" said he at once.

"Not a scratch," said I. "Where's Rose Noble?"

"Up stream, I think," said Mansel, climbing into the boat.

Then he bade me go up to the gallery and expect him and Rowley again in ten minutes' time. When I asked him where he was going, he said, "To bestow the boat."

When I was up in the chamber, I was not surprised that he had asked me if I was hurt, for, though there was little disorder, blood was all over the place. We afterwards learned that this came from Rose Noble's head, which I had cut open – most likely with the first tin I threw. And this shows how tough the man was, for all his grossness: for the tin must have weighed three pounds, and I flung it with all my might.

Hanbury had little to tell, beyond that, as Mansel surmised, he had lost his way in the dark and, horrified at hearing my shots, had made at once for the junction to see what was there towards. There he had found Ellis and Job and the tanner and another he did not know. Ellis was raving about the escape of the Rolls and vowing most shocking vengeance against whosoever it was that had cut the ropes; and the four then appeared to be watching the road and the river, in observance of some design he could not comprehend. He had seen the two flashes from the woods, as also had they; and it was Job who had at once repeated the signal. Not long after that, the windows of the gallery had suddenly been illumined, to Hanbury's horror and the great surprise of the thieves, who seemed too much dumbfounded to utter a word, though the tanner and his fellow let out at once a flood of excited talk. Then Hanbury had left them, to hasten in fear and trembling down to the water's edge, where he had run into Mansel, himself hot-foot for the boat.

And there, when Mansel returned, he took up the tale.

"Rose Noble was in a boat, moored in mid-stream. I believe he was there all the time. In his eyes the Rolls was a plum, of which he would have been very glad; but our pit-head was the very pie itself. So Ellis was given the job of taking the Rolls; but Rose Noble took on the business of locating and seizing the pit-head.

"It was Punter, I imagine, that heard us, as we were sculling down stream, and gave the signal which Hanbury saw Job repeat.

"Rose Noble must have been beside us, whilst you, Chandos, went up and Rowley came down. But, being as shrewd as they make 'em, he held his hand.

"So much for speculation.

"I've had some shocks in my life, but the sight of those windows lighted hit me between the eyes.

"We made enough noise embarking to be heard for a furlong or more, but Ellis and Co., I suppose, had no ears to hear. There was no room for Rowley, but he laid hold of the painter and swam behind.

"We missed friend Bunch by inches. I suppose he had lost his direction, for he was sculling down stream. So we came to the shoot. When I saw this was shut, I decided to go for the trap as fast as we could.

"We dropped down stream and landed below the road of approach. I'm afraid we must have broken all Punter's 'marks' but that couldn't be helped. Whilst I was forcing the door of the kitchen-hall, George and Rowley ran to the well for rope. They were back with a coil and a blanket before Bell and I had withdrawn the second slab.

"When we were down, we could hear no sound at all. The light we had seen was gone, and I don't mind admitting that I was deeply concerned. Now a torch always makes you a target;

yet I felt I must have light: so I sent Bell off for the searchlight without more ado.

"What then happened you know. But for your warning, Chandos, Rose Noble must have shot me dead.

"As it was, the tables were turned.

"Hanbury sat down in the ramp with the searchlight between his knees; and I took my stand behind him, ready to fire.

"I fancy Rose Noble knew that the game was up.

"To bring us within his range, he was bound to enter the beam, and the moment he entered the beam, he would be certainly blinded and almost certainly shot.

"By way of rubbing this in, I audibly requested Hanbury to advance a couple of feet.

"A moment later I heard him go down the shoot."

Whilst we were eating some supper, I told my tale over again; but, when Hanbury and I would have discussed the future, Mansel checked us with a yawn.

Then he laughed.

" 'Sufficient unto this day is the evil thereof.' Rose Noble has gone far enough towards murdering sleep. Don't let us finish it off."

Then he told Bell to lay his bed, when he made it, across the flap of the shoot.

"I don't see how they can lift it," he added slowly; "but tonight has shown me that I don't know a risk when I see one, so from now on I'm going to turn every stone."

And then and there I happened to look at my watch. At first I made sure it had stopped, but, when I had checked it with Hanbury's, I found it was telling the time. This was five minutes to twelve. And since we had been at supper for half an hour, my passage with Rose Noble cannot have taken up more than ten or twelve minutes of time. And that, but for its proof, I never would have believed.

Soon the lights were put out, and we lay down to take our rest; but for an hour or more I could not slumber for thinking, of those ten or twelve minutes and how close to death I had come.

And here let me say I was sorry for Rose Noble, for, unconscionable villain though he was, he deserved to have won that trick. To enter the gallery, as he did, was a great accomplishment, and, but for the failure of his torch, he must, I think, have brought us all to our knees. Yet, all he got for his valour was a broken head.

8

The Race for the Chamber

The next morning we held a short council.

The system of reliefs, which had served us so long and so well, was now a thing of the past, and we were all agreed that, once we had closed our bases, except to communicate with Carson or to go out as a spy, no one must leave the dungeon until the treasure was won.

That the stranger whom Hanbury had seen was the tanner's brother we had no doubt, and, to judge from the fellow's demeanour, so far as we were concerned, the two were at one with the thieves; if this were so, since they were the innkeeper's allies, our enemies now numbered eight, instead of five.

Yet, neither of these conclusions troubled us near so much as the thought that Rose Noble must know that there was a second entrance into the *oubliette*. This was a serious matter, for, now that he knew, he would not rest till he had found it, and, as if that were not enough, we had left him a definite clue. Rowley had covered our tracks as best he could, but he could not repair the door which Mansel had forced; its broken condition the thieves were bound to remark, and, the instant they saw it, they would know that the entrance they sought led out of the castle itself. "And so," said Mansel, "it's only a matter of time. It may take them a day or an hour, but in the end they'll find it, and then the balloon will go up."

Now, if we guarded the trap, though they found it, to force an entry that way might be very hard, for three men armed, in the darkness, could hold it against an army similarly equipped. But what a man has done once, he will do again; and we had little doubt that, if we opposed their entry, they would at once resort to the use of that terrible weapon which they had already employed, that is to say, bombs; and stand up to these we could not, if for no other reason, because against such an attack no man born of woman could hope to hold such a place. We could bar the postern of nights, we could set an electric alarm above the stile, we could keep watch: but more we could not do, and must try the fortune of war when the moment came. But Mansel decided that in future we must always go armed, even though we were working at the nose of the shaft.

It was then arranged that the next morning I should go to the culvert, and, taking the Rolls from Carson, send him back to the dungeon and myself drive to St Martin for the last time.

"You see," said Mansel, "at the moment we're not up against Time; but I shouldn't be surprised if we were, before the curtain comes down. Give me five minutes' start, and I'll be at Calais five hours before Rose Noble; but not if I've got to trip round, paying my bills. So we'll do three more reliefs. When you've bade farewell to St Martin, Hanbury can visit Villach; and then I can go to Salzburg and make all smooth and clear for us to withdraw. I think we should each go alone, because four's none too many to hold the fort. And I think we'll have Tester here; he'll rather like this place, and he'll be devilish useful, watching that trap."

With that we talked no more, but went to work, Mansel and Hanbury to setting the electric alarm, and Rowley and Bell and I to driving the shaft.

Thirteen days had gone by since we had altered our course, and so well had we wrought in this time that but twenty-three yards lay between us and what we had come to call "live ground." We gave it that name, because, though we knew it was surrounding the chamber, as a garden a house, we were far less certain where within it the chamber lay. We hoped and believed that, by holding straight on through this region, we should strike some part of the chamber before we had gone five yards; we were equally sure that, if we had not found it in nine, this would be because we had passed it; and, in such an event, we proposed to go no further, but to drive a new shaft at right angles through the middle of the live ground. We had made up our minds that this region was not more than nine yards square, and we steadfastly refused to consider that somewhere within its area the chamber did not lie.

Whether the progress we made was actually swift or slow I cannot fairly pronounce, for how six sextons would have fared, had they been set such a task, I cannot say. But what we lacked in experience, I think we made up in zeal; and, after all, digging is a simple, downright business, which one man, if he will, can soon do as well as another. Be that as it may, I do not think any men could have laboured more heartily than we had, since our brush with the tanner upon the ninth night of June. But now, since our life was to be less easy, we determined to cut our confinement as short as ever we could and to that end to redouble our efforts to reach our goal. We had not much hope of so doing before the thieves discovered the trap; but there was a chance that we might, and, faint though it was, this certainly spurred us on, for, although we were ready enough to show our teeth, once such a battle was joined, no one could possibly tell what the outcome would be.

And there, of course, the thieves had a valuable advantage; for, if one of them was wounded, the others would let him lie or die for want of attention, rather than care for him to the cost of their enterprise; but, if one of us was hurt and needed a doctor's aid, everything else, of course, would go by the board.

In this sense the dice were loaded, and, though hitherto we had been most fortunate, this spectre always haunted each passage of arms that we had.

Full of these thoughts, we worked as hard as we could, and by the end of that day had actually advanced five yards, so that but eighteen remained between us and the live ground.

At one o'clock the next morning I left for the culvert, charged by Mansel to swim down the middle of the river and not to attempt to land for a quarter of a mile. I was then to strike across country and by no means to use the road, until I had left the junction two miles behind. Directly I had found Carson I was to send him back, for else it would be broad daylight before he could reach the shoot. "Indeed," said Mansel, "I'm banking on your meeting by half past two, for Carson is sure to be early and so, I think, are you, for the culvert is less than four miles as the crow flies. Tell him on no account to let Tester off the lead and to hold the end in his mouth as he swims to the shoot."

I was at the culvert at half past two and had just found the note which Carson had lodged in the brickwork under the arch, when I heard a step above me, and there he was.

Two minutes later he and Tester were gone, and I was turning the Rolls.

There was little to do at St Martin, except to collect my belongings and pay my bill. But I had to explain how it was that I came a day late and alone and without the basket which my hostess had so often put up. I might have found this hard; but, between their relief to see me and their distress to learn that I should return no more, the good people seemed to have no room left for surprise. Indeed, I might have been a fugitive monarch, resting at the house of a loyal subject before resuming his flight, for they could not do enough to show their esteem and goodwill. And, when at last I left them, I had to give them my word that I would one day come back, and, even so, enough honest tears were shed to make me feel ashamed that I had imposed so much on their simplicity.

Hanbury met me at the culvert, but had nothing at all to report, save that another five yards had been added to the length of the shaft. And, by the time he was back on the following day, we were within eight yards of the live ground.

We were all glad of Tester, and Tester was glad of us. He soon understood that, when there was no one to spare, he was expected to guard the *oubliette*, and I think he enjoyed wandering about in the darkness – for now we burned no lights, except in the gallery and at the nose of the shaft – and conducting an endless scrutiny of the great banks of earth. The shoot seemed to fascinate him, and he always contrived to be present, when its flap was withdrawn. I fancy he thought that it must have been made by some beast and was continually hoping that its creator would emerge.

When Carson took his leave, I could not help wondering when we should see him again, for, with Mansel's return, the last of our reliefs would be over, and, if all went well, the next time we crossed the river would be the last. He was very loth to leave us and constantly lamented that he had not killed Rose Noble on the night when we visited the well. "One minute more," he would say, "and I should have had him cold. And that would have saved us a peck of trouble, sir, for, if ever I saw one, there goes a dangerous man."

Be sure I agreed with him. And yet I must honestly confess that, if we had suddenly learned that the thieves had withdrawn, the game would have lost a curiously attractive savour, which even the lifting of the treasure would not have wholly restored. For danger, once you have tasted it, is a superlative spice.

If Carson was loth to go, we were sorry enough to lose him, for he was a fine workman and a first-class shot. What was more, he had the brain of a fighter and, though there might be no one to lead him, could be trusted to think for himself and to hold his own.

However, neither Rowley nor Bell could manage a car as could he; besides which, it was good to know that our line of retreat was held by such capable hands.

His instructions were clear.

So soon as he reached Salzburg he was to lay up the Rolls and, taking the second car, drive her to Villach. There he was to bestow her at the inn which Hanbury had used, and then to return by train in search of the Rolls. After that he was to go no more to Salzburg, but to take up his quarters at Villach, holding both cars in condition to leave at an instant's notice by day or night. Each night at eleven o'clock he was to be at the culvert and, having concealed the Rolls, to wait there till twelve. He was then to walk to a point a mile and a half away, where seven trees grew together on the top of a hill. From here could be seen the castle and a slice of the river below. If he saw nothing unusual, he was to go his way; if he saw one window lighted, he was to return to the culvert and wait till we came; if he saw two illumined, he was to leave the Rolls and come to the shoot; but, if all three were aglow, he was to get the Rolls and drive down, past the junction and on to the Lerai road.

We had little to report to Mansel, beyond that our progress had been slow. For, since he had left, we had only advanced three yards, because we had encountered a boulder as big as a sheep, the dislodgement and disposal of which had taken the best part of five hours. But, if, instead of progressing, we had actually retired, I do not think Mansel would have cared, because he was so much relieved to find that the secret of the trap was still inviolate and that we had not, in his absence, been called upon to fight for our lives.

That day we made a great effort; and by eight o'clock that evening we had reached the coveted region and had broken the live ground.

Our excitement now began to run high, and I was for bolting my supper, in order to get back to work; but Mansel said he should like to visit the combe, and me to go with him.

"It may seem idle," he said: "but those who don't look don't see. To visit the well or the castle would take more time than I think we can fairly spare; but to go to the combe and back will take us less than an hour. I hope and believe it will be our last reconnaissance, but I think we ought to make it before we take off our coats for the final push."

And so we went out together, when it was dark.

Hanbury told me later that, when we returned, Mansel was rather pale, but I looked an older man. I have no doubt I did; for, although we had seen no one and heard no sound, what we had found was enough to age any man who thinks the fruits of his labour worth taking up.

At the foot of the gutter we had found a miniature lake.

Now, whilst we were drawing water, we had never gone down to see the pool we had made, and, though we all remembered the sodden condition of the ground on the day I was taken by Ellis, that was nothing to go by, for then no water had been drawn for eighteen or twenty hours. We had, therefore, the bare fact before us that the enemy was making for the first time a truly formidable effort to empty the well – a feat which we had accomplished in less than three days. How long they had been at work, how much water they had drawn, how the results of their labour were comparing with those of ours we could not so much as guess; *but what six men had done eight men could do*; and this indisputable verity, sternly illustrated by the lake at the foot of the combe, bade fair to sap the resolution from which our endeavours sprang.

I can only speak for myself, but I know that, when I was back in the gallery, I felt tired and was glad to sit down and that, when Bell brought me dry shoes, the business of changing seemed a burden and I told him to put them down and let me be.

Then I heard Mansel laugh.

167

"Rose Noble leads," he said lightly. "And yet I'll back the old firm. There's the straight to be covered yet, and I fancy they're full of running. Besides, I don't know how you fellows feel, but I haven't shovelled dirt for six weeks for the pleasure of watching Rose Noble pick my peach. Then again, the game's the thing.

"And now let's see where we stand.

"As yet they've not got to the shaft. That is clear, for that water was drawn today, but the gutter was dry, which means they've stopped work for the night. If it was over, and they'd found, there wouldn't be so much water at the foot of the combe, for once they've uncovered the shaft, they've only to bail to keep the water down; and five hours' bailing wouldn't make all that mess.

"Again, I know they're eight; but only four will draw water as fast as we: and one of those – Rose Noble – has something better to do, for you can't command such a rabble and bear a hand as well. Besides, I'll stake my oath that, water to draw or no, Rose Noble's still trying to find the way to the *oubliette*. And I think it more than likely that they're keeping an eye on the shoot.

"And last of all, they none of them know of the bars. And that's a fruit of a thought, for I'll lay my soul to a cesspool that, apart from anything else, they're short of a file."

With that, he ordered Rowley to open a case of champagne, "for, though," said he, "I meant us to drink it when the treasure had been won, now that I come to think, we might not have time, and it seems a pity to leave it for Ellis and Rose."

I can relate his words, but I cannot describe the way in which he spoke them, or the quiet, confident manner with which he seemed to be putting Misfortune to shame.

Enough that he lifted us up and carried us all away.

And, since neither Hanbury nor I would wait for the wine, Mansel himself brought a bottle to the nose of the shaft and made us drink.

We worked straight through that night, and it was eight the next morning before Mansel called a halt. By then we had tunnelled four yards into the live ground. This had meant working at a tremendous pace, for we faithfully maintained its dimensions and propped the shaft as we went. The heat was awful, and the want of air most vile: but we had grown used to these conditions, from which we had begun to suffer as soon as we turned the shaft. Still, we came down into the gallery, swaying like drunken men, and Hanbury and Bell fell asleep over their food.

Then Mansel told Rowley and me to take our rest and said that he should take Tester and sleep in the *oubliette*. I believe he said something else, for I remember laughing, but before my laughter was over I was asleep.

Now how long Mansel slept I do not know, but he woke us at noon, to say that he had sunk a crowbar at the nose of the shaft and had encountered water four feet below its floor.

Except that he had found the chamber, he could not have brought us more encouraging news, for it showed that we had, at least, no vertical error to fear and that, roughly, our floor was level with that of the chamber itself.

In a moment, therefore, we were wide awake and afoot and all agog to return to the nose of the shaft. But of this Mansel would not hear, until we had all of us bathed and broken our fast.

"Method in all things," he said. "Disorder never won yet and never will. We went off the deep end last night, but we're not going to do it again. From now on we'll labour by shifts; there'll always be four at work and one at rest. I don't know how much we can stand, but it won't be for long, and four hours on to one off seems the most convenient rule."

And, whilst we were eating, he outlined what must be done to cope with a sudden attack.

"The one who is off duty must sleep in the *oubliette*. Tester will wake him all right, in the event of attack. The moment he's waked, he will withdraw to the ramp – of course, taking Tester with him – and close the postern gate. And he will hold the ramp, while the others will hold the shaft. In this way we shall have them between two fires, and, if we don't loose off too soon, it ought to be a walk-over."

Then he told us to mind how we went at the head of the ramp, as well as at the mouth of the shaft, because he had built two breastworks out of some sacks of earth.

"Why, you can't have rested at all," cried Hanbury.

"I had two full hours," said Mansel, "and now I'm off to have one more. Chandos, what time do you make it?"

I told him twenty past twelve.

"I shall be your relief," said he. "I count upon you to wake me at half past one." I suppose I hesitated, for he continued at once. "Unless you give me your word, I shall not sleep."

"I promise," said I.

"Very good," said Mansel. "But if, before then, you strike oil – well, I don't mind being called early to hear the news."

Five minutes later we were at the nose of the shaft. We had still five yards to go, before we should come to the end of the belt of live ground, but, though we went steadily forward, we now took to searching right and left, by dint of driving a crowbar, as though it were a great nail, into the wall. Again and again, by this means, we thought we had found the chamber, but when we had laid bare the obstruction, each time it proved to be some boulder or two or three smaller stones. In this way the tunnel began to lose its symmetry, and, though this could not be helped, the propping of the roof with timber became a less downright business and wasted a lot of time.

We worked frantically, speaking very little, but doing the best we could to maintain the system of labour which should turn to the best account such joint strength as we had.

The hewer stood on a sheet on to which his winnings must fall. As soon as these began to encumber him we would stand back and away; at once his assistant would draw back the sheet from the face and lay in its place another to catch the next fall of earth. The assistant then disposed of the soil he had drawn away, and by the time he was back the second sheet would be full. The carpenter followed the hewer as close as he could, pitching his uprights and cross-bars and wedging them into place; and the fourth was man of all work, now shovelling loose earth that had fallen clear of the sheet or had not fallen, now helping the carpenter, and now bringing up fresh wood.

An hour before his relief, each man had a pint of champagne, and, when he was waked, was given a quarter of an hour in which to bathe and eat. Mansel fed Tester himself twice in the day, and that was all the attention the poor dog had, yet he was as good as gold, never obtruding himself as so many dogs would have done, but seeming to know that we were fighting with Time and faithfully keeping to his post in the *oubliette*.

By eleven o'clock that night we had advanced five yards and were clear of the live ground.

It was impossible not to be disappointed and very hard not to be dismayed. And, when I had called for a crowbar and, with three mighty blows, slammed this up to its head into the nose of the shaft, *and touched not so much as a pebble*, I think we all avoided each other's eyes.

But Hanbury – for Mansel was resting – wasted no time. By his direction we immediately withdrew five yards and began to drive a new tunnel out of the left-hand wall.

For no reason that I can offer, the half hour that followed seems for me to stand out of that period of toil and trouble; and I remember most vividly the sob of the hewer each time that he launched his pickaxe and the smell of sweat and the blinding glare of the searchlight and even a mark on a timber retaining the left-hand wall. To our right, the five yards we had won to no purpose continually mocked us, like the Psalmist's bulls of Bashan, gaping upon us with its mouth; to our left, our long, clean-cut gallery seemed to be leading fantastically into another world. I can see Hanbury poising the compass and hear him curse as his sweat fell on to its dial; and, when Bill who was hewing, missed his stroke, I remember snatching the pickaxe and missing mine.

So the work went on, and the niche in the left-hand wall had grown to an entrance, when Hanbury looked at his wristwatch and cried that my time was up.

I stumbled back to wake Mansel and fell asleep in his stead, for the champagne had done its business and my knees were beginning to sag.

Almost at once Hanbury woke me, and I started up with a cry.

"Have you found?"

"Found be damned," says George. "You've had five minutes over your time."

So it was with us all; and we battled rather than laboured, fighting with nature, like madmen, in our effort to find the chamber before she could wear us down. For the pace was too hot to last; we all knew that; and unless we could win very soon, we were playing a losing game. Yet we went steadily on, like men in a dream, losing all count of Time and confusing Night with Day. Indeed, the demands of the battle so wholly possessed our senses that, used in some other direction, these were beginning to fail. We shouted, one to another, when a whisper could have been heard; the hand that could still ply a hammer, could not be trusted to raise a glass to the lips; and, if ever I glanced at my wristwatch, this seemed a great way off.

At a quarter past nine the next morning, our new shaft was eight yards deep. And this alone shows that we were beside ourselves, for, though we had cut down the width, relying upon the crowbar to make this good, such progress was superhuman. Yet, to advance this shaft further seemed little worth, and we started another tunnel out of its right-hand wall. This was by Hanbury's direction; for Mansel was resting and we others knew no more where to turn than the man in the moon.

"Are you certain," said I, "that we're not too far to the left?"

"Certain," said Hanbury. "Mansel will bear me out. The shaft from the well to the chamber is not so steep as we thought, so we've aimed too much to the right. You mark my words, if you don't strike the chamber this time, we shall hit the shaft."

Such confidence did us good, but when I roused Mansel, I saw him tighten his lips, and I knew that he had been hoping to be sent for before his time.

I now know that I must have slept for nearly my hour, when I dreamed I was listening to Mansel broadcasting news and that a storm somewhere was blotting out what he said. I must have dreamed for some moments, for I was heavy with sleep, but at last awoke, to find Tester barking like fury three feet away.

In an instant I had caught him up and had blundered through the postern to fall headlong over the breastwork with the dog in my arms. However, I was up in a moment and made haste to close the gate; but I dared not fasten it closely, for fear of a bomb.

I had much ado to quiet Tester, who was seething with wrath; but, when I had done so and could listen, I heard no sound.

So we lay still for five minutes; then I heard Mansel's voice.

"Are you at your post, Chandos?"

"I am," said I.

"What happened?"

"I've no idea," said I. "I woke up to find Tester barking, and that's as much as I know."

"Stay where you are," said he.

Then he unmasked the searchlight and turned the beam on to the trap. Presently he raked the dungeon, letting the beam discover the timber and piles of earth.

At length –

"Let Tester go," he said. "And you come in."

The dog ran to him at once and jumped up to lick his face. Then he turned away and began to growl and bristle, *with his eyes on the trap.*

"Not much doubt about that," said Mansel, stooping to make much of the dog. "Our friends have found the front door. I suppose they're not quite ready, and that's why they shut it again. Well, we're quite ready when they are, and till then, we may as well work."

Then he sent me to bathe and eat, and, when I came back, Hanbury was asleep in the dungeon, with Tester in the crook of his arm.

We gave no more time to the riddle, for in truth we had none to give. The business smacked of a nightmare; yet, our present life was a dream; and so, if we thought, we did not speak of it, but tacitly took it for granted that Mansel's interpretation was good.

At six o'clock that evening we started another shaft.

The last we had driven five yards, and had sunk a three-feet crowbar into its nose. *And found nothing.* And so at six o'clock we started another shaft. This was driven from the nose of our second, so that our original tunnel would soon be a left-handed fork with three five-yard prongs.

And here I am bound to record that we were beginning to fail. I will swear that the spirit was willing, but the flesh was beginning to flag. It was nearly forty-five hours since Mansel and I had returned from our reconnaissance, and, though in that time we had each had ten hours' sleep, the reconnaissance had come at the end of a full day's toil. We had, therefore, been jaded when we began to spurt, and our spurt was losing its sting, because it did not end.

We were beginning to fail.

I knew that my strength was failing, and tried to conceal the fact. I fancy the others did the same, for the collapse of one must mean the end of our effort. The camel's back would have broken; not even Mansel could have carried another straw.

When I roused him at half past seven, he held up two canvas kit-bags for me to see.

"The Burglar's Delight," said he, with half a laugh.

I tried to laugh back, and lay down – but not to sleep. And there was the surest sign that the end was at hand, for it showed that the flesh was rebelling against its chastisement.

When Mansel returned from the gallery, he stopped to peer at me. I pretended slumber; but his action showed me that he, too, had not slept.

I think the hour that followed was the worst I have ever spent. I was so sick and weary that I would have sold a kingdom for unconsciousness; but this was steadfastly withheld; and, though at times I fell into a kind of doze, this state was more dreadful than my first, for then my brain was unruly and flitted and gambolled, as a gnat on a summer's eve.

I was, indeed, thankful when Hanbury limped into the dungeon and I could go back in his place.

The gallery we were now driving was completing the uppermost prong of the letter E, the upright of which was formed by our second shaft and the base, or bottom prong, by the last five yards of our first. But, because of all our sounding, the works had a shapeless look and seemed to reflect the frenzy with which they had been done. The roof and walls were eccentric, and the timbers were all awry; indeed the carpenter's task was now fit work for a wizard, and faithfully to prop and retain such irregular excavation was almost impossible.

At half past ten that night our new shaft was two yards deep. Mansel, Hanbury and I were working alone, for Bell had just left to rouse Rowley and take his place. And all was quiet, for Mansel had stopped for a moment to drink his wine, Hanbury was pencilling a timber, which he was going to saw, and I, who was hewing, was extracting a morsel of dirt, which had made its way into my eye.

At first I thought Hanbury's pencil was making a scraping noise; then I saw he had stopped and was listening and that Mansel was doing the same.

For a moment no one of us moved.

Then Hanbury stepped to my side and set his ear to a hole which the crowbar had made a foot back in the left-hand wall.

"That's right," said he, after a moment. "It's coming from here."

Then he stood away, and I made play with the pickaxe about the hole.

I had soon made a hollow, in which by sinking the crowbar we should gain another foot; but, before we did this, Mansel tore off his zephyr and folded it into a pad which should muffle the sound of the blows.

Gently I drove the bar home, and could almost have pressed it for the last foot of its way; and I drew it out with my hands without any effort at all.

The noise was distinct now – a thin, regular murmur as if someone was whetting a chisel upon a hone.

What it was I could not imagine, and was just beginning to think that our calculations had led us to the top of the well, when Mansel let out a sob and caught us each by an arm.

"*My God, I've got it,*" he cried. "*That's the chamber ahead.* AND THEY'RE FILING THE BARS."

There is, I believe, a height at which a man's heart will break; and so, I suppose, there is a pitch of excitement at which a man's brain will balk. And I think we had come to this, for Mansel was trembling as a man smitten with an ague; if I had tried to speak, I should have broken down; and, while we were standing thus silent, Hanbury's knees sagged and he fell down in a swoon.

The faint was nothing, and, before I had brought the bucket which was standing ten paces away, George was again on his feet; but we made him dip his head in the water, and then Mansel and I did the same.

Then we fell to, like madmen, to deepen the breach I had made.

We worked in what silence we could and let the carpentry go; each of us hewed for two minutes, while the others withdrew his winnings and strewed them about the shafts; now and again we had to employ the shovel, but mostly we used our hands, so as to make less noise.

All the time the noise of the filing went steadily on, only ceasing from time to time to instantly recommence. Each time that it stopped our hearts went into our mouths; for, close as we were, if once the bars were severed, we might have been five miles off for all the good we could do.

When Rowley came back, we told him and sent him back to tell Bell.

"And say," said Mansel, "that I may not arrive when I should, but that, whatever happens, he must remain where he is; for now the case is altered, and he and Tester are holding our line of retreat."

Rowley was back in two minutes and wild to take his turn, and, once he had got it, he would not surrender the pickaxe, and I had fairly to wrest it out of his hands.

Now what the time was when it happened I do not know – for I cannot tell to an hour how long we took to cut through that last three feet – but I know that I launched the pickaxe and its head went out of my sight and that there I was, looking through a hole into an empty space, beyond which, when they gave me the light, I could see a stone wall.

It was the chamber indeed.

At once I saw that the well-diggers' excavation had been bigger than the chamber itself and that they had not lined the cavity which they had dug, but had built the chamber within it, like a box within a box.

There was now no mistaking the whine of iron biting iron, and it sounded to our frantic ears as though whosoever was filing was nearing the end of his task.

We, therefore, fell to, like fury, and soon had a ragged window, I suppose, some three feet square, opening into the cavern in which the chamber stood.

A moment's inspection now showed that the chamber was round, like the well, and was plainly constructed of stones which had been cut by the masons to build the walls of the well. To break out of the chamber, therefore, would have been ten times as simple as to break in; for the stones were undoubtedly wedge-shaped, and, that being so, if they were truly laid, a battering-ram itself would not avail us. The joints, moreover, were as fine as those of the walls of the well, and to cut out one stone with a chisel would have taken an hour or more.

"What of the roof?" whispered Mansel.

At once I stretched up an arm, to find the roof just out of sight, but two minutes' work with the pickaxe had laid the edge of it bare.

Now how the roof was constructed I do not know, but between the slab we could see and the stones upon which it was resting, there was a layer of mortar as thick as a Camembert cheese. And this was so loose that I picked out a piece with my thumb.

Here, then, was the way to break in, for we had but to drive a chisel, and, when it was fairly in, to lever against the slab, to prize a stone out of the wall, and, once one stone was out, we could make our breach.

"And, when we do," breathed Mansel, "look out for squalls; you can bet your life they're not going to give us this trick."

We had to make for the lever; so once more I handled the pickaxe, whilst the others marshalled the tools for the final assault.

All this time the filing continued, and, to judge from the ring of the metal, some bar was nearly in two. Indeed, as I threw down the pickaxe, again the noise stopped, and we heard some blows administered, as though the workman believed he could burst asunder the filament that remained.

We waited to hear no more.

I fitted the edge of the chisel into the chink; and, whilst I held it, Mansel hammered it home.

The stone below must have been loose, for, the moment we levered, it yielded, and a second later I pulled it out with my hands. The two below came away, and, as Hanbury gave me the searchlight, I heard a strangled cry.

On the tiny floor was a bag, thick covered with dust, of the shape of a sack of corn. Its mouth was shut, but one of its sides was gaping and spilling the stuff it held. By its side was another; but this was all gone to ruin, and its contents lay in a heap. The dust lay so deep over all that it might have been trash, but I saw the shape of a crucifix standing up out of the ruck.

Immediately opposite was the entrance, barred by the four iron bars. Behind these I saw two faces, unshaven, like those of beasts. The one I had never seen, but the other was that of Ellis; and that I believe I shall see so long as I live, for if ever the devil possessed the soul of a man he possessed it then.

The other seemed blinded by the searchlight, but Ellis glared full at the lamp, as though it were no more than a taper, with his face working with passion and his eyes staring out of his head.

Suddenly he laid hold of the bars and wrenched them this way and that, screaming, like some animal with rage; and, when they would not yield to his frenzy, he clapped his face up against them and spat like any demoniac, lending the whole force of his body to this disgusting act. Then he started, as one who recovers his presence of mind, and I saw a hand fly to his hip.

At that moment Mansel fired, and the fellow fell suddenly forward against the bars. As he did so, the other man turned, and Mansel fired again. But, when the noise had subsided, we could hear him descending the shaft.

Then Ellis' body slipped sideways, till the head was against the wall, which held it up at an angle which was different to that of the trunk.

"God forgive me," said Mansel, "but I'd do it again."

With that, I climbed into the chamber, and Mansel followed me in.

With the hammer and crowbar, we soon had three more stones out, and Hanbury made his way in.

Then Mansel told Rowley to give him the canvas bags.

"And *Quick*'s the motto," said he. "I missed the tanner, and now he'll give the alarm. But, once we're beyond the postern, they can have the *oubliette*."

Rowley had brought the bags and was standing without the chamber, looking in, with his hands on the wall, when I heard a rustle behind him and saw him drop suddenly forward across the breach we had made.

A mass of soil had broken away from the "window" and had fallen on the back of his legs.

He was not hurt, but was pinned; and, whilst I supported his body, Mansel and Hanbury climbed back into the tunnel and shifted the fallen earth.

They worked feverishly; but two or three minutes went by before he was free and I was able to help him into the chamber.

"And that," breathed Mansel, brushing the dirt from his hands, "is about as clear a time-signal as ever there was."

I held one canvas bag open and Rowley the other, while Mansel and Hanbury shovelled the stuff within. There was gold and stones and jewels and all manner of lovely things, but I think we were thinking of safety and the way to the *oubliette*.

Then Mansel lifted his head and touched Hanbury on the arm.

For a moment we knelt there, listening.

Then, something faint, but clear, came Tester's vigorous bark.

And that was the only time we heard him give tongue that night, for the next instant came a shuffling and then a rumbling sound; and, when we had brought the searchlight up to the breach in the wall, had we not known its angle, we could not have told where the shaft we had driven had been.

"Where's the pickaxe?" said Mansel quietly.

I told him it had lain in the shaft.

Then came another rumble and the searchlight went out.

9

Out of the Eater

Had our doom been set forth upon paper and submitted to Rose Noble himself, for his approval, I cannot believe that he would have altered one particular.

We were entombed alive; this, by our own act, with the treasure under our hand, in the knowledge of an attack upon one man and a dog, who would count in vain upon our succour.

Had we had the tools, we had no longer the strength to hew our way back; indeed, to judge from the sound, it seemed likely that ten or more yards of our tunnel had fallen in. Yet, could we have performed this unthinkable task, it would only have been to fall into the enemy's hands.

And the other way out was barred; and beyond the bars was the shaft, the mouth of which would be sealed in less than an hour; and beyond the shaft was the well, some ninety feet deep.

Mansel was speaking.

"The first thing to do is to keep calm: the second is to break these bars. And now please don't move for a moment, or we shall collide."

We heard him make his way to the entrance; when he was there, he spoke again.

"Chandos, come here and lift Ellis. If I can find it, we may as well have his torch."

At once I moved to the entrance and, thrusting my hands between the bars, seized the corpse under its arm and endeavoured to lift it up. But it was too heavy for me, so Mansel and Hanbury raised me, whilst I held it against the bars.

The torch was alight in a pocket, into which the dead man must have thrust it, so soon as he heard our chisel enter the wall; and, when Mansel had taken it out and had felt in the other pockets, he told me to throw back the body away from the bars. This I was thankful to do.

The entrance was a frame of hewn stone, eight inches thick. In this the bars were set upright, four inches apart; and, close to its foot, one was filed almost through.

We cut this in two with the chisel without delay; but, if we then expected that our release was at hand, we were grievously disappointed.

God knows what smith it was that wrought that bar; but he was a craftsman that knew his mystery; and I do not believe that such art is practised today.

Severed though it was, we could neither break nor bend it: and, when we attempted to lever it up with the crowbar, we bent this into a loop.

There lay the file within reach, but we could not bear the thought of a labour so lengthy and cudgelled our weary brains to find out some other way.

Now the bars were all sunk, top and bottom, into holes cut in the stone, and, though our treatment had not displaced it, the upper portion of the bar we had cut could now be turned round in its socket and even moved up and down, and, but for the lower portion, which opposed it, it would have come down and away. Perceiving this, we determined to loosen the lower piece, in the hope that we could then raise this up, until it was clear of its bed, and thus remove the whole bar, by simply reversing the procedure by which it was undoubtedly set up.

It did not take long to loosen the lower portion, but, either because the stonework itself had settled or because, when the bars were planted, some trick of masonry was used, we could not make enough play to free this piece from its bed.

The knowledge that the water below was rising fast and that the mouth of the shaft would soon be sealed made it hard to give our minds to the problem as freely as we would have wished and easy to return to methods which we had already discarded as forlorn. And this, I suppose, was the beginning of panic. Be that as it may, I remember Mansel sitting down with his head in his hands, whilst I leaned against the wall, holding the torch and watching Rowley filing like a madman and Hanbury, with the hammer and chisel, trying to cut a channel out of the stone.

Suddenly –

"Look here," said Mansel rising. "Why don't we try the wall? It let us in, and why shouldn't it let us out? And, once we're out, we can break our way into the shaft."

We should, of course, have attempted this long before; but I suppose it was natural that the entrance, so nearly open, should have attracted and held the whole of our attention. But now we saw that, provided the void we had found ran right round the chamber, we should be outside in a moment and very probably able to make our way past the entrance without having to displace any earth. For the entrance was two feet wide, but the shaft was three.

And so it fell out.

In less than five minutes, six more stones were out of the chamber's wall, and, when I stepped through the new opening, there was the wall of the shaft twenty inches away. To breach this was very simple, yet took longer, I think, than even Mansel had expected; for we had ruined the crowbar and dared not work too fiercely for fear of spoiling the chisel or snapping the helve of the only hammer we had. But at last we had made an opening through which a man might pass.

While Mansel and I had been working, Hanbury and Rowley had put what remained of the treasure into the bags and had fastened their mouths. This by Mansel's direction, "for," said he, "I know that a man can take nothing out of this world, but, so long as he's in it, he may as well keep what he's got."

And there we were all with him, for, when you have staked your life on some adventure, it is a bitter business only to save your stake.

So we escaped from the chamber into the shaft, taking the bags with us.

There was a rope fastened to one of the bars. I suppose it had been bound there by the tanner, to enable Ellis to make the ascent of the shaft; but it stood us in very good stead, for the steps were very irregular and covered with slime.

It was at once arranged that we should descend one by one, for, rope or no, it was not a place to play tricks in, and, if two used the rope together, one, by slipping, might bring the other down.

I went first, dragging a bag behind me, and, when I had reached the water, Hanbury followed me down.

The water was roughly one foot from the top of the mouth of the shaft, and I could see a pale radiance which I knew for that of the moon. The air, too, was fresh, and, chill and dank as it was, because of the depth of the well, I can never describe the relief I found in breathing it, and I think it did more to refresh me body and soul, than anything that had happened since Mansel and I had found the water at the foot of the combe.

So it was, I think, with us all. And of such, I suppose, is the way of Providence; for, if ever four weary men had need of comfort, we needed it then.

Except for a plank, floating upon the water, the well was as empty of gear as a blown egg.

I do not think we had counted on anything else: we had, rather, deliberately, refrained from leaping, so to speak, until we were come to the ditch. But we had hoped desperately to find something – some rope or scaffolding which would have given us a chance, if not of scaling the walls, at least of rising with the water and so avoiding the most miserable of deaths. But there was nothing at all, and, though I went out with the torch and, getting astride of the plank, recklessly raked the walls for as far as the torch would light them – and that was some thirty feet up – I might have spared my labour, for they were as bare as my hand.

"Nothing?" said Mansel, as I came back to the shaft.

I shook my head; and, as they helped me ashore Hanbury and I, between us, let fall the torch, and there was an end of that.

For perhaps two minutes we stood, with our eyes on the water, already full four inches higher than when I had seen it first ten minutes before.

Then I heard Mansel catch his breath.

"What fools we are!" he cried. "We must be losing our minds. What was the use of this plank without two beams? They're not afloat, because they're locked in the niches, but I'll lay a monkey we find them two feet down."

With that, he dived and, after what seemed a long time, came up with one of the rafters which Carson and I had cut from the outhouse roof. In a moment I had the other, and together we set them in the niches which were now two inches above the water line. Then we laid the plank across them, and, five minutes later, the four of us were standing upon the stage.

We had had a struggle to bring the bags out of the shaft, for they were immensely heavy; indeed, we had almost lost one; and this made us so uneasy that Hanbury went back to the shaft and cut a length from the rope and, with this, lashed them loosely together, so that they could hang from a beam, as a pair of saddlebags slung on the back of a horse.

We did not sit down, for the plank was nearly awash and very soon we should be able to raise the stage, but, as I have said before, all the way up the well the niches lay two feet apart, and, the beams being heavy and we having nothing to stand on, but only the water itself to buoy us up, we could not raise the rafters as much as two feet at a time, but must wait till the water had risen and made this distance less.

So we stood in a row on the plank, and, when the water was half-way to the calf of my leg, we raised the stage.

Again we had a battle to save the bags, for to keep afloat ourselves during the transfer was almost as much as we could do, and swapping horses in mid-stream must be child's play compared with the struggle we had to raise ourselves and our baggage twenty inches above the flood.

But at last it was over, and we were again on the plank, with nearly an hour before us before we must move again.

Enforced inaction, I suppose, never helped anyone. But, sitting there in the darkness, we had nothing to do but think. And, when I set down my thoughts, I think I am revealing more or less what was in each of our minds.

Our state was melancholy.

We were as cold now as, a short time before, we had been hot. We had to chafe our fingers, to prevent them from growing numb. Mansel was stripped to the waist, and we were all drenched and dripping and utterly worn out.

Of succour from without, there was no hope at all. Carson was miles away, and Bell, if indeed he was not dead or captive, was holding the postern gate.

The water was rising at the rate of thirty inches an hour: but this pace would not last for long, and *twenty-seven hours must elapse before we could climb above the high-water mark.*

And, if by some miracle we could endure so long, if, before then, the thieves had not returned to the well, to find us waiting with the treasure, what then?

Then we should still be thirty-four feet from the top...thirty-four feet...

We had been confronted with three apparently insuperable steps. First, we had been locked in the chamber; yet we had escaped. Then we had been trapped in the shaft; yet we had emerged. And now we were down in the well. That is to say, we had taken two of the steps, only to find that the third was insuperable indeed.

I will not say that there was no more spirit in us, but the figures with which we were faced would have daunted anyone. Twenty-seven hours of waiting; twenty-five several battles to raise the stage; and then – thirty-four feet which, unless some rope was dangling, we could not possibly scale. And when, after thirty minutes, Hanbury rose to his feet and said quietly, "I'm sorry but I can't stand this," I think we all understood.

"I'm going to try to climb up," he added gravely, "by means of the niches."

"Steady, George," said Mansel, laying a hand on his arm. "The thing's impossible. No one in our condition could bring it off."

"I'm going to try," said Hanbury. "It may be a chance in a million – "

"It isn't that," said I. "The niches come to an end ten feet from the top."

There was a long silence; and presently Hanbury sat down.

And how long we sat still then I cannot remember, but I know that all of a sudden Rowley, who was sitting beside me, gave a great start and then began to laugh like a man at a play.

I laid hands upon him, for I thought he had lost his wits. But as soon as he spoke I knew there was nothing to fear.

"I'm sorry, sir, but it's like a clown in a ring. We'd sell our souls for a ladder, and *we're sitting on one all the time.*"

There was a moment's silence.

Then –

"Put it more clearly," said Mansel. "I believe I see what you mean."

And that, I confess, was more than I could have said.

"The beams, sir," said Rowley. "We can set them above one another, and then, when we're all on the top one, pull out the one below and lift up that. And so on. I know there'll be ten feet to go, sir, when we get to the top, but it's better than waiting until – until we can't wait no more."

"It is, indeed," said Mansel heartily. "Rowley, I give you best. And when we get out, *as we shall*, I'll thank you for saving my life."

Then we all spoke at once and laughed and jested and clapped Rowley on the back, as if we were souls in a tavern and full of ale, instead of upon the brink of the most hazardous endeavour that ever four wretches made.

Then Hanbury slipped off the plank into the water, and the rest of us straddled the beam over which the kit-bags hung; and when he had freed the other, he gave it to us, and we fitted it into the niches two feet above.

Happily the beams were on edge, or they would not have borne our weight; but, before ten minutes were past, we would have given a fortune to have had a third. Whether the plank would have helped us, if we could have cut it down, I do not know, but the chisel we had left by the chamber, and there was a foot of water above the mouth of the shaft. And since it could not have carried us, though it might have served as a rail, we let it go.

When George had climbed out of the water, before we went any further, we determined exactly the system by which we must go. "For," said Mansel, "if ever an exercise required a military precision, this is the stunt. We've only to make one mistake, and we shan't be in a position to make any more."

The first thing which we decided was to preserve the order in which we sat on the beam. Mansel was sitting at one end, and Hanbury at the other, each of them facing the wall; I was next to Mansel and facing the same way as he, and Rowley was next to George; and the bags hung in the middle, between Rowley and me.

And, for the sake of convenience, I will do as Mansel did then and number us off; so that he became 'Number One,' I became

'Number Two,' Rowley became 'Number Three,' and Hanbury 'Number Four.'

Numbers One and Four were to move and take their seats on the beam we had just set up. They would then take hold of the niches two feet above, to gain what stability they could. Numbers Two and Three would then move and, between them, lift up the bags, before moving up themselves. When they were up and in place, Numbers Two and Three would lean down, keeping their balance by holding to One and Four, and, laying firm hold of the beam which was resting below, would draw it out of the niches and lift it up. They would bring it as far as their shoulders and there lay it down, when Numbers One and Four were to guide it home.

That was our method; and, though, looking back, I think we might have done better, the devil was driving, and so it had to serve.

Now at first all went like clockwork, and we must have climbed twenty-six feet, before the depth below us began to make itself felt.

I think we had all perceived that here was the serious drawback to Rowley's plan, for the highest niches were nearly eighty feet up; but it was so important that we should not lose heart that no one had even hinted that a fear of falling might presently supervene.

Be that as it may, I know that all of a sudden the palms of my hands were dripping and I was afraid to move. Rowley and I, between us, had lifted the bags, and he had just taken his seat on the upper beam, but I dared not change my position, for I knew that, if for one instant I were to release my hold, I should not be able to regain it, but must inevitably fall.

By Mansel's direction, I waited; and, after two or three minutes the attack seemed to pass away: but, a few minutes later came another, and everything had to wait until I recovered my nerve.

I suppose my head was the weakest, for I was the first to show fear; but presently Hanbury asked us to give him two minutes' grace, and, when at length he moved and I turned to lift the bags, Rowley began to tremble, and five more minutes went by before he could play his part.

From then on, the ascent was a nightmare.

If we had had a third beam, it would not have been so bad, but the rafters were very narrow and to bestride the upper, without any handhold above to help us to keep our seat, sometimes required such an effort as we could scarcely make.

Again, it would have been better, if we had not had to look down, but the dark motion of the water was constantly catching the eye and reminding us of the doom which one false movement would evoke.

My hands ran so fast with sweat that I was continually fearful of letting fall the rafter which Rowley and I were to raise; and once, when my end was free, but his would not leave its niche, I had to let go of Mansel and put down my other hand, because, if I had not done so, the beam must have slipped from my grasp.

We dared not rest, if for no other reason, because the depth below us seemed to feed upon delay; for, so often as we waited for someone to recover his nerve, the bare idea of moving seemed to become monstrous and the renewal of the struggle a hazard we could not take.

With this increasing horror came other fears, and, though we spoke hardly at all, I think we imagined vain things. Now a beam seemed to be bending and now insecurely lodged; we supposed one beam to have fallen, and saw ourselves trapped in mid-air; we wondered if one of us fell, what the others would do; behind all, the ten nicheless feet to which we must come rose like some sinister cliff where the wave of endeavour should be stayed. But, while these apprehensions were transient, the height at which we were working was always there, and, what was worse, growing more obtrusive with every move we made.

Yet we went on somehow, making our way up the well, building our ladder as we went.

I do not remember feeling weary, but only most stiff and sore; and, indeed, I find it astonishing that we managed so well as we did; for, before we had located the chamber, we were almost dead-beat, and, when we were sitting on the plank, I was so much exhausted that, if I had fallen off, I am sure I should have sunk like a stone. Yet, though we were not sprightly, we moved with a will, and I think it must have been our nerves that kept us going, for I do not believe that we had any physical energy left.

After a long time we could make out the top of the well, for the light of the moon had vanished, and it was very dark. And, with this, a new dread came to plague us, namely, that the thieves would return before we were up. And at times we made sure we had seen the flash of a torch, and at others that Rose Noble was waiting and only letting us carry the treasure up.

We had moved, I think, thirty-six times – but I cannot be sure – and I had just taken my seat, when Mansel spoke.

"This niche is my last," said he. "Hanbury, do you say the same?"

After a moment – "Yes," said Hanbury.

"Very good," said Mansel. And then to me "Carry on."

So for the last time Rowley and I withdrew and lifted the beam: and Mansel and Hanbury guided it into place.

Then Mansel stood up and straddled it and ran his hands over the wall; and Hanbury did the same. But neither spoke, and presently both sat down.

"William," said Mansel, looking up, "are you sure we're still ten feet down?"

"Certain," said I. "I've marked it many a time."

"Well," said he, with a sigh, "I'd rather be ten feet down than thirty-four. Can anyone see the chain?"

We could make out the windlass, but no one could see the chain. "Let's hope it's dangling," said Mansel, "three or four feet away."

With that, he and Hanbury descended and sat on the lower beam; then they withdrew the upper and gave it to me, and, while they and Rowley crouched down, I turned the timber crosswise, in the hope, if it was there, of striking the chain. But I encountered nothing, and after a moment or two I was thankful to give it up and to hear it slide back into place.

Then for a while we sat silent, continually gazing upward at the rim of the well.

And then at last I perceived the only way. And, wet with sweat as I was, when I saw it, I broke out again. But it was the only way, and, after a little discussion, we made the attempt.

Mansel and Rowley bestrode the upper beam, this time facing each other, instead of towards the wall. I stood between them, in the middle of the lower beam. When they were ready, I put my hands on their shoulders and mounted the upper beam, and, when I was standing upright, I let myself fall forward against the wall. This was but three feet away. At once Hanbury mounted behind me and stepped up on to my shoulders. This brought his head to the level of the rim of the well, and an instant later he was up and within the redoubt.

In a flash he was at the windlass and had let go a length of chain. Then he locked the windlass and, pulling the chain in by hand, lowered it so that it hung between my face and the wall. I seized it easily enough, and one minute later I was out of the well.

Then we hauled up the bags and Rowley and, finally, Mansel himself. And, when he was up, with one consent we all lay down on the ground, and no one of us moved or spoke for five minutes or more. To tell the truth we were past speaking; and I cannot set down our emotions, because, even at this distance of time, I can find no words which can tell our gratitude and relief.

So we all surmounted the third insuperable step, and, thanks to Mansel and Rowley, found ourselves risen from the dead. For Mansel brought us into the well, and Rowley taught us how to climb up, and, though they both made much of what Hanbury and I had done, I am afraid the depth of the well lent our performance a glamour which it did not deserve.

The redoubt was deserted.

For this we were thankful; yet it quickened our concern for Tester and Bell; and, when I remembered Rose Noble's way with a hostage, I felt uneasy indeed.

We were, all of us, streaming with sweat; so Mansel took a shirt and a jersey, which he found hanging up, and each of us took some clothing against the cool of the night.

Then we passed into the meadow and took to the woods.

We dared not go by the castle, but bore towards the shrine, presently turning left-handed across the road of approach. So we came down to the river, which we made at a point not very far from where Mansel had hidden the boat. To find this took us some minutes, for, although we could see the dawn coming, it was still very dark. But at length I fell into a gully; and there it was.

Then Mansel gave Hanbury Ellis' pistol, which he had taken from the body before he descended the shaft.

"You and Rowley," he said, "stay here and hang on to the bags, while Chandos and I take the boat and scull to the shoot. What we shall find I know no more than you; but whatever happens, I think you must both sit tight, for I know I'm too tired to swim, and we've been close enough to drowning for the last three hours. And, as soon as it's light, I think I should dry that pistol as best you can."

With that, we launched the boat, and at once I bent to the sculls.

When we came to the shoot, we listened; but, except for the lap of the water, we could hear no manner of sound.

Then Mansel took his pistol and, withdrawing the magazine, took out the ammunition and wiped it dry. There was a round in the chamber, and he dried that as well. Then he reloaded the weapon, and, when it was quite to his liking, he put up his hand and rang the bell.

For a moment or two we sat waiting.

Then the flap was withdrawn.

Now whether it was Bell who had withdrawn it or one of the thieves we could not possibly tell; if it was one of the thieves, now was the moment to enter, as Rose Noble had done; but whoever it was did not let down the ladder, and Mansel dared not demand it, because at once his speech would give him away.

Suddenly, to our great joy, we heard Tester let out the grunt which he kept for matters suspicious, whose claim to be passed in silence had yet to be proved.

"Bell," said Mansel at once.

"Sir," said Bell.

"Where's Rose Noble?"

"In the *oubliette*, sir. There's four of them there, *an' the innkeeper's pulled up the rope, so they can't get out.*"

"But the postern?"

"Carson's holding that, sir. When you didn't come, I thought I'd best bring him here."

"Well done, indeed," said Mansel. "And now let down the ladder, and I'll come up."

Then he gave me his pistol and told me to pick up the others and row them across the river, treasure and all.

"And then come back here," said he, "as soon as you can; for this is the last lap, and, between you and me, I've a fancy to win the race."

With that, he went up the ladder, and I sculled back to the others as fast as I could.

Hanbury and Rowley could hardly believe my news; and, indeed, to me it seemed almost too good to be true, for that Bell and Tester should be safe smacked of the supernatural, but that Rose Noble should have permitted himself to be snared was almost inconceivable.

I was back at the shoot in ten minutes, and at once Bell lowered the bucket full of our clothes. Then he let down food and wine, and, lastly, a medley of things – arms and papers and money and *Lockhart's Life of Scott*. Finally, he descended and proposed to row me across and then himself to return for Mansel and Carson. But I had him across the river, before he had got his clothes, and, when he had unloaded the boat, I sculled back for the last time.

I arrived to find Carson throwing down our last coil of rope, and, after a little, he descended, with Tester under his arm. Almost at once the rope-ladder fell into the water, and, an instant later, Mansel slid down the shoot.

He would not enter the boat, but laid hold of the painter and bade me bend to the oars.

So soon as we were ashore, we sank the boat; and, two minutes later, we all set out for the culvert, bearing our treasure with us, like men in a fairytale.

The dawn was up, but we held to the road, for to make our way across country was beyond our power. As it was, we lurched and staggered, and once I fell asleep walking and, taking no note of a bend, fell into the ditch. Yet Mansel drove us on, "for," said he, "I'm not going to be caught at the post. There's the postern and the shoot and the river between them and us; but four of us are no better than dead men, and I couldn't hit Rose Noble at seven feet. And there you are. I'm sorry to spoil your outlook, but we've got to be in France before sunset, and there's quite a long way to go."

At last we came to the culvert.

There we left the rifles, bestowing them under the arch. And then, without more ado, we all climbed into the Rolls, and Carson drove us to Villach as fast as he could.

There we only waited to take up the second car; and Bell was set to drive this, because, after Carson, he was the least fatigued.

Ten miles short of Salzburg we stopped; and, when we had done what we could to order our appearance, we emptied the Rolls' tool-box and packed within so much of the treasure as we could make it hold. It was a capacious coffer, but, when it was full, there still remained a good deal: most of this we hid in the tyre of one of the two spare wheels, and what was still left we concealed about ourselves.

All this because of the Customs; for we knew very well that, if it was found at a frontier that we were laden with jewels, we should be certainly stopped and those in authority informed.

And here, for the first time, I perceived that, though we had lifted the treasure, we stood in imminent danger of losing every ounce; for if once its existence came to the knowledge of the State, all the resources of the Law would be employed to prevent six foreigners from abstracting so considerable a fortune.

This peril shocked me so much that I besought Mansel to wait and to let us dispose the treasure in some less conspicuous place. But he would not listen.

"I dare not wait," said he, "because of Rose Noble. I'm not afraid of him, because now we've had some sleep; but I don't want a brush with him in a public place. Whatever the outcome was, explanations would have to be made. *And we're not in a position to explain.* Nobody is, when he's carrying stuff like this. As for the Customs, we've as good a chance there today as we should have next week. I shan't enjoy the passage, but it's got to be made. As far as the tool-box is concerned, I'll give you an excellent rule, if you've something to hide, always hide it in the most obvious place. And now don't worry. If you can't go to sleep, look inexpressibly bored. And please try not to perspire. Perspiration is the emblem of an uneasy mind."

If that was a true saying, the officials who dealt with us were an unobservant lot, for, while they examined the Rolls, the sweat ran down my face. But Mansel paid the dues with an injured air, and, after a little delay, they let us pass.

So we entered Germany; and at half past five that evening we came to France.

And here I thought all was over, for they turned us out of the car and took up the cushions and carpet and opened the petrol-tank. They did not open the tool-box, *because they saw Mansel do that.* I saw him do it, too, and thought he was out of his mind. He took out one of the rubbers with which we had covered the treasure and then put a foot on the tool-box and started to dust his shoes, talking politics all the time with the Frenchman in charge and becoming so engrossed in his discourse that the search had been done and we were back in the car, before he had finished his dusting and put his rubber away.

And, when later we spoke of the matter with bated breath, he merely observed that prevention was better than cure.

"But you must have been worried," cried Hanbury.

"Worried?" said Mansel. "I think it took a year off my life."

And there you have Jonathan Mansel.

Master of many things, he was especially master of himself. His self-control was so perfect that those who knew him best could no more read his heart than they could look through a plate of armour of proof. Add to this that he could think twice as swiftly as other men, and you will see the disadvantage at which his enemies stood. When we were in any trouble, because he was wiser, he saw more clearly than we the depth of the risk we ran; yet he was always the coolest, the most confident, the most matter-of-course. With it all, he was never secretive. All his movements were gentle; yet he had the strength of two men. He was most unassuming and generous: yet was most plainly revered wherever he went.

I never knew, till long after, that, when he became lame, as the result of a wound, he lost his balance and so his head for heights, and that, from that time on, it troubled him to so much as look down from a balcony on to a garden below. Yet on that awful night he came up the great well and gave no indication then or at any time of the agony he must have suffered from this terrible thorn in the flesh.

At Strasbourg we turned South, and, when we were deep in the country, we took a little by-road which led to a wood. There we spent the night. And at eight o'clock the next evening we reached Dieppe.

So I came back to England the way I had come some seventy days before, with the dog-collar in my pocket and my heart in my mouth.

And here, before I go any further, I will set down Bell's tale.

He had heard the trap open, for he had not been asleep, and he and Tester had at once withdrawn to the ramp. No bomb had been thrown, but four men had at once descended into the *oubliette*. One of these was Rose Noble, and another the tanner, for he had passed close to the postern, and Bell had observed the odour which hung about him. Almost at once they had all gone into the shaft. They were a long time gone, and, before they came back, someone else had descended and followed them in.

Suddenly Bell had heard the unmistakable cry of a man in terror of death. This came from the shaft.

At once a spout of German had burst from the trap, and, since he could hear two voices, Bell knew that they must be those of the tanner's allies. Their tones were plainly apprehensive, and again and again they repeated the name "Johann," and at last Bell gathered that the cry must have come from the tanner and that *the two at the trap were suspecting foul play.*

Sure enough, when the thieves returned, as they presently did, and Rose Noble commanded the landlord to draw him up, the latter demanded "Johann," and, when the thieves sought to bluff him, made it plain in pitiful English *that he and the tanner's brother would take no one of them up until they heard "Johann's" voice.*

Now what in the world we were doing Bell could not tell, but supposed we were holding the chamber, instead of the shaft, and, since, if they could not get up, the thieves were certain to try to force the postern, he decided to summon Carson to help him to hold the ramp.

He, therefore, whipped down to the gallery and, opening two of the windows, turned on our electric light, and then sped back to the postern to witness a turbulent scene, the thieves roaring orders and threats, and the innkeeper and his companion hurling down taunts and abuse. Then somebody fired at the trap, and at once, as though in answer, the rope came tumbling down on to the stile.

Then Rose Noble had turned upon Punter and rent him for leaving the trap, and Punter had cursed Rose Noble for taking the tanner's life. But Rose Noble declared with an oath that the tanner had hoaxed them.

"He's done in Ellis," he said, "and the bags are down in the shaft. He was meaning to box us here and then go back with his fellows and pouch the lot. And, if we don't get out of this hole, those other two black-blooded rats will have it yet."

"But where's the Willies?" cried Job.

The question confounded Bell, but appeared to sober the thieves; for at once they lowered their voices, clearly believing that we were all in the ramp and presumably fearing that we should leave by the shoot and make for the well.

Presently Job had approached and endeavoured to force the postern, and, while he was so engaged, Bell shot him dead.

At once the other three had retired to the shaft, from which Bell fully expected that we should soon drive them out. But when presently Carson arrived, yet there was no sign of our coming, he could not think what had happened and began to fear very much that some accident had occurred.

200

When Carson heard his story, he had at once decided that Bell must have taken some rest and that, if in three hours' time, we had not appeared, they must force their way into the shaft, to see what the trouble might be. But, before that time had expired, we had come to the shoot.

Four several times the thieves had approached the postern; but, I suppose, no one of them was minded to give his life for the other two; for a frontal attack alone could have been successful; and that they did not make.

In the hope of reducing their number, Carson had held his fire as long as he dared, but, though he had wounded Punter, they gave him no other chance.

So, in the end, Rose Noble's astonishing instinct overleaped itself; for, had he not slain the tanner, finding the fellow guilty of something he had not done, he must, I think, have had the treasure and four of us into the bargain.

There is little more to be told.

On the way from Newhaven to London we stopped in a lonely place and put the treasure back into the canvas bags. And, when we reached Cleveland Row, we carried it up and laid it in Mansel's flat. And there, for the first time, we saw what it was we had won.

The spoil was that of a robber of high estate.

There was nothing common, and, except for a small bag of gold, no coinage at all.

There were jewels of all descriptions and many loose precious stones. There were brooches and clasps and circlets; there were cups and the hilts of poniards, studded with gems; there were two crucifixes and a monstrance and the crook of a pastoral staff, the presence of which, had he been charged with sacrilege, Axel the Red might have found it hard to explain; there was a golden chessboard, with ruby and emerald chessmen, as fine as you please; there was a scourge, the seven cords of which were loaded with seven diamonds, the size of full-grown grapes; there were jewelled dice and bracelets and eighteen or twenty rings; there were images and girdles and a golden hunting-horn; but most lovely of all was a triptych, whose three little, sacred pictures were done like stained-glass windows, only with precious stones.

When we had examined it thoroughly, we packed it all into a plate-chest and lodged it at Mansel's bank.

And there, I suppose, our adventure came to an end.

Most of the treasure we sold, but Mansel, Hanbury and I each kept some one of the gems. They made me take the triptych, because the secret of Wagensburg had been bequeathed to me. And I have lent it to a Museum, because, to be honest, I dare not house it myself.

For what we sold we received nine hundred thousand pounds, "which is very much less," said Mansel, "than what it is worth; but that cannot be helped, for I never was any good in the counting-house, and, from what I've seen of you two, you're worse than I." And, indeed, for my part, if I had been told it was worth but half a million, I should have been none the wiser and perfectly content.

Of this huge sum Mansel, Hanbury and I took each two ninths for himself; and Carson, Rowley and Bell received one ninth apiece.

To my great surprise, when Bell had been given his cheque, he said that, if I was content to keep him, he had no wish to leave my service; when I pointed out that he was now a man of means, he said that, for his part, that did not alter the case; and since Hanbury and I were proposing to share an estate in the country, I told him to take a holiday and report to me in three weeks' time.

Both George and I found it hard to part with Mansel; and, when the latter suggested that we should come down to Hampshire and spend a week with him there, we were only too glad to accept.

And there, in the midst of the New Forest, he brought us back to the world; for our doings of the last two months had thrown our focus out, and, when we looked upon the future, this seemed intolerably grey. But Mansel pointed the virtue of quiet enjoyment, maintaining that only those who knew the quality of peace could, when the moment came, taste the full flavour of battle; "for," said he, "for the last two months we have been against the peace, and that is a condition which is all very well for a time but, if it is too much prolonged, will surely lose its sweetness and, what is infinitely worse, will sour the years that are left in the cellar of Life."

So he did us an enduring service, for, but for that week in Hampshire, I do not think that either George Hanbury or I would have ever settled down, but, having the means to do so, would have gone out to rove the world in search of more excitement and so have dropped substance for a shadow and thrown our birthrights away.

As it is, I can now look back upon those seventy days as a man regards some picture, the contemplation of which never fails to bring him infinite delight, for they stand clean out of a quiet, orderly existence and, by the contrast, gain immeasurably.

Their burden is as vivid today as it was that sunshiny morning when we unloaded the tool-box, not far from the London road – the murder of the Englishman, and the quiet contempt of his prophecy that Ellis would come to grief; the level-crossing, and the fierce pounding of my heart as we sat awaiting the train; the courtyard of Wagensburg, and Mansel against the lime-tree with Rose Noble stretched at his feet; the ear-splitting crash of the bomb, and Mansel's steady voice calling the roll; the heat of the closed car's engine scorching my back; the smell of tanning, and Tester's menacing bark; Rose Noble's weight upon me, and his heavy breathing as he set out to take my life; our last, stupendous effort to reach the chamber, and Ellis dead and staring against the bars; and then, our terrible battle with that most jealous of wardens, the great well.

The memory of these things I find as valuable as my share of the treasure itself, and I doubt if ever a man was so well paid for undertaking the care of a masterless dog.

The latter is with me always, and I think her life is happy. I have called her "Rafter," for, as the name of a dog, the word does well enough, while it will always mean a great deal to me.

And here I may say that Tester was more fortunate than she, for he never went into quarantine, but, instead, into the tool-box of the second car, to emerge upon Ashdown Forest with, to judge from his spirits, a new lease on life. But, then, he was a hardened smuggler, and had cheated the Customs this way a dozen times.

Dornford Yates

As Berry and I Were Saying

Reprinted four times in three months, this semi-autobiographical novel is a humorous account of the author's hazardous experiences in France at the end of World War II. Darker and less frivolous than some of Yates' earlier books, he described it as 'really my own memoir put into the mouths of Berry and Boy', and at the time of publication it already had a nostalgic feel. A hit with the public and a 'scrapbook of the Edwardian age as it was seen by the upper-middle classes'.

Berry and Co.

This collection of short stories featuring 'Berry' Pleydell and his chaotic entourage established Dornford Yates' reputation as one of the best comic writers of his generation and made him hugely popular. The German caricatures in the book carried such a sting that when France was invaded in 1939 Yates, who was living near the Pyrenees, was put on the wanted list and had to flee.